Long Sleep

The Novel of
Your Nightmares

Melissa Saari

Van Rye
PUBLISHING

Cover design by Vila Design

Published by Van Rye Publishing, LLC
Ann Arbor, MI
www.vanryepublishing.com

ISBN: 978-1-957906-04-1 (paperback)
ISBN: 978-1-957906-05-8 (ebook)
Library of Congress Control Number: 2022940604

Contents

Chapter 1

OPHELIA CARTER HEARD a man chuckling behind her as she stood at the river's edge. "There are more things than you can imagine in the water," the man's voice said to her.

Ophelia turned around to face the river, where many people were dunking their feet in the water while others built sandcastles in the dampened sand. But none of the people were looking at her, and none of them were grown men like the voice. They were mostly just small children like Ophelia. She glanced back at her parents, but curiosity and heat quickly drew her attention back to the cool water.

"Don't worry, the water's fine, Ophelia. It will cool you off," the male voice repeated. Ophelia's parents kept talking about church, too busy to notice her walking off. "Come and swim in the water," the voice continued. "It's perfectly safe, and it will cool your body."

"Who are you?" Ophelia asked while walking toward the water.

"It's safe, you'll see," the voice said. "Let me cool you off, my child. I'll take care of you now. Just come closer."

The moment Ophelia's sandals sunk into the cool water, tendrils of cold ran up her calves and took her breath away. The water covered her calves and then her pink shorts. With

1

every step, she felt less dizzy, and tingles of coolness rushed up her torso. Soon, only Ophelia's head stuck above the brown water. The water cooled the air in her lungs, and she felt heat escaping from her shoulders and head.

"What are you waiting for?" the voice asked. "Dunk your head! Break free of the heat!"

Ophelia submerged completely and became lost in the muddy water. Even if she had dared to open her eyes, she wouldn't have seen anything. Deep beneath the river's muddy waters, no light dared to reach.

"The light shines in the darkness, and yet the darkness perceives it not," Ophelia heard the voice say while she was underwater. She thought the voice sounded like one she knew—that of Pastor Henry. But she couldn't figure out how his voice could follow her under the water.

Ophelia pushed her arms back forcefully, dragging them in small crooks to reduce the backflow, then putting them into a strong push to force her forward, and then another crook. With every stroke, heat escaped her body in luxurious-feeling waves. Jubilant, Ophelia kept swimming underwater until something hard, like a rock, slammed against her forehead.

The slam broke Ophelia's concentration. For a moment, she felt tremendous pain in her forehead. And then, Ophelia's soul left her body in a single rush.

Chapter 2

EVERYTHING CHANGED WHEN Ophelia went to the other side. There wasn't a shimmering staircase like everyone said there would be. Instead, there was dark, like the night sky, and purple dots floated past her. Ophelia felt a sensation of being pulled upward, though no light broke through the darkness to give her reference.

The purple dots floated away and were replaced by white streamers, some shooting right past Ophelia and then some right through her. A large circle of white light emerged above her, growing larger, and she realized she was going into the circle. She expected some sort of impact, but the transition to a land of lavender was effortless and didn't cause her any pain.

An endless field of purple lavender sprigs flowered at once, bursting forth in dazzling color. The ground was alive with color from horizon to horizon. The evil presence that had tempted Ophelia into the water was long gone. Its cloying, soothing presence no longer clouded her mind. She felt completely at peace.

The scent of lavender flooded Ophelia's nostrils, cleansing every pore and refreshing her spirit. She had never experienced this sort of bliss before; she had only heard about it in church. She wasn't sure where the waves of scent came from, but once she felt at peace, the waves no longer buffeted her. Instead, they calmed her and held her in a serene moment. She was flying through the sky without even a bird for company, but she could sense she was not alone.

"Where am I?" Ophelia asked out loud. Flying above the violets made her feel like Peter Pan. She took a long breath in through her nose, and the smell of lavender filled her with peace again.

With delicate movements, Ophelia twirled forward. Although she could see the lavender beneath her, she couldn't begin to guess how far away it was. The horizon faded into white, and the lavender seemed identical in size from one end of her view to the other. The field of lavender mesmerized her, and her eyes searched for some pattern in an ocean that seemed to reveal none. Flying across the meadows, Ophelia relished her new skills and twirled through the air in outrageous curlicues.

"Oh, child, there is so much more that has importance in the world!" said a loud female voice that seemed to come from all around Ophelia.

"Who said that?" Ophelia asked. But her only answer was waves of joy that echoed through her lungs and made a buzzing vibration in her head. *The voice must be in my mind*, she thought.

Ophelia stopped twirling and tried to make her body hover, with the cloudless blue sky above her and the realm of lavender flowers far below her. Then, a beam of white light pierced up from the lavender, spinning the flowers in a spiral beneath. At the same time, Ophelia felt a rush of air against her face that pulled her attention from the floral display. She looked up to find an angel before her.

Ophelia had no doubt that this was an angel because, from the apparition's back, two gigantic wings reached out to each side of her. The wings were flapping once a second in a pendulous swooping motion that started at the wingtip. A thought crossed Ophelia's mind: *If that's an angel, does that mean I'm dead?*

Ophelia's soul already knew the answer, so she did not have to ask the angel. As Ophelia continued to hover but sank closer to the lavender, the angel rose even higher above her. "Are you taking me to God now?" Ophelia asked the angel, with fear in her voice.

The angel was taller than the adults back on Earth. She flew above Ophelia, pushing her towering wings in confident pulses. The countless feathers pulsed three times before the angel spoke again.

"It's wonderful to meet you, Ophelia! It's an honor; it truly is. My name is Paivatar, the Guardian of the Chosen Ones. Don't worry, child. You're in God's hands now! You can't die—not when you still have so much to accomplish!"

Ophelia felt confused. "What do you mean?" she asked the angel. "I'm too young to have a purpose yet. Am I being punished or something?"

"Now is not the time to be shy, Chosen One! I've been trying to reach out to you since the day you were born."

Doubt fled Ophelia's mind as she listened to the angel. All the great "chosen" people she knew about had terrible things happen to them before they were brought up into the glory of God. "I've never been chosen for anything," she said. "Have

5

you met every Chosen One before me?"

"Oh, of course, child! Buddha met with me. Jesus visited me at one time. But you had to die to meet me, so your case is a little more extreme. Your power comes directly from God because you're so close to him right now. And even when you return to the world, your soul will still be close to the Lord."

As Ophelia kept hovering in the air, she asked, "Did you let me fly because I'm the Chosen One?"

"Absolutely not," Paivatar said, laughing. "All souls can fly. Didn't you know that? This is not the time to be asking foolish questions! You don't have long to linger in Heaven."

"Pastor Henry says that spirits have to stay on the other side. They can't break through to Earth. He said something bad would happen if they did. So, how can I possibly go back?"

"Don't be afraid. You're surrounded by divine power now. This is where I've watched over you since the day you were born, singing songs of your praise every morning. This is where you'll receive your powers, and this is where you will be when your life is over. I'll keep watch over you for the rest of your life, and the demons will never break through my vigil."

"Why did I never hear you before?" Ophelia wondered.

"Because you've never died before," Paivatar explained. "I've never had a chance to show you. Now, you can learn your healing powers—the ones you were meant to have the day you were born. Please focus, Ophelia. We don't have much time."

"What was the name of that demon who killed me—the voice I heard?" Ophelia asked.

"It's better if you don't know since even thinking his name can summon him. Don't even think about the sound of his voice. You will learn not only the power to heal wounds of the body but also the mind. You'll reach within people's minds and change nightmares into good dreams."

"How can I do all that? I don't have any training at all!"

"Just reach out to people with your mind and know that your body is protected by my divine vigil. Now, still your mind and receive the blessing of the healing touch so that your soul can't go back to your body."

Ophelia pushed her hands out just a few inches, and Paivatar put her hands around Ophelia's. Warm, healing, golden light poured into Ophelia's hands. As the light filled her hands, she saw her arms beginning to glow, and then her legs, too.

The energy pouring into Ophelia had healing properties. As it flowed through her, new pathways wove through her body, allowing the healing energy to be processed. Inside Ophelia's mind, old thought patterns, telling her how worthless she was, drifted away and became idle to make room for the healing intentions she was learning. The process of absorbing the energy became an education as she felt her old assumptions fade away, replaced by crystalline knowledge. Truth from a divine power—pure knowledge—splashed through Ophelia's mind like water sloshing down a waterslide.

Although Ophelia's old ideas were hard to let go of, they all flew from her mind like troubled birds, and she never saw them again. Replacing them were visions of the human body— male and female, side by side—while strong filaments of light bound together Ophelia's internal organs and bone and skin. In brilliant rainbow light, the energy wound through Ophelia's body, and she learned that this glowing light was the mind pouring through the body.

In blinding visions, Ophelia suddenly saw how she could dive into the filaments of light in her body to plunder people's dreams. Dreams, in the form of bubbles, poked through the light, and Ophelia could see inside each bubble.

In mere seconds, Paivatar was giving Ophelia glowing medical lessons and primers on dream manipulation. Ophelia learned more in seconds than most monks learn in decades of meditation while bathed in the light of God's majestic wisdom. The knowledge of healing that Ophelia gained was so profound that it broke through all her religious preconceptions.

The light now enveloping Ophelia was brighter than anything she'd ever experienced in her short life, and it was causing her to have trouble focusing on the lightning-fast lessons she was absorbing from Paivatar. Deep inside her spiritual body, Ophelia felt groundswells of power that she had never felt before. She knew at once that what was flooding her—being given to her—was God's healing power. And once Ophelia's new healing powers had flooded her entire body, she felt invincible.

"I'm seven years old!" Ophelia cried out. "How can I be ready to wield this kind of power? I'm too young!"

"You've *always* been ready, sweet child," Paivatar reassured her. "You've had to watch people suffer before without being able to help them, and it pained you. I saw it. Isn't that true?"

"Of course," Ophelia confirmed. "Yes, I've always wanted to help people."

"Well, now you can bring healing to those people, and the

world will be changed forever. The energy I've given you is for other people, not yourself. So, when you come back to life, you will feel exhausted in spite of your new powers."

"You're actually going to bring me back to life?"

"Not me, child. It's the human beings on your miraculous, unspeakably beautiful planet who are working to bring you back to life as we speak. In a moment, you will be in agony but will soon be restored to full health. And once you are, anytime you need to use your new powers to heal someone, I will be right by them so that you know it is time for healing. Now that you're being given a second chance at life, you must prove to everyone else that God really can work miracles so that they stop doubting him. What higher calling could you possibly want? Now, return to Earth—you've already lingered here too long!"

Ophelia held her peace, too astonished by the revelations to ask any more questions. And this seemed to satisfy Paivatar. "I will guide you every step of the way," Paivatar assured Ophelia. "But hurry! You have stayed here too long already. You must go back now!"

"How?"

"I've warned you, Ophelia. You can't stay here too long. Go back!"

A huge rush of wind made Ophelia's head hurt, and she felt herself falling. The falling sensation continued, and she hurtled into the lavender. Excruciating pain shot through her body. Ophelia thought the pain came from the lavender, but when she opened her eyes and saw the paramedics, she knew it was the pain of coming back to life.

9

Chapter 3

"I'VE JUST ABOUT had it with Father Henry!" Caroline Thompson said.

"What do you mean?" Julie White asked while crossing her arms. "He's a man of God! Don't talk about him like that."

"Well, he doesn't have a backbone, Julie. He stands there and acts like nothing's going on when those teenagers use their cell phones in the middle of his service!"

"I'm sure he talks to them after the service," Ethan Carter chimed in while reclining deeper into his beach chair. "That's the sensible thing to do, isn't it? To not shame them in front of others?"

"But he also chased some homeless kids away from the church the other day!" Caroline shouted. "Is *that* a sensible thing to do?"

"Hey, did you hear about that party, Ethan?" his wife, Marilyn Carter, asked while nudging Ethan in the elbow.

"No. What party?" Ethan asked. He threw back the rest of his wine and poured some more for Marilyn and then himself.

"Sally Decker is throwing a party at the Baptist Church the day after tomorrow. We should head down there." Marilyn took another long sip of her white wine. "I can't wait to show off one of my famous desserts!"

"You don't *really* want to go to Sally's party, do you?" Ethan asked after another long drink of wine. "I heard her making comments about your casserole, saying that you don't know how to keep the cheese from singeing on top." Ethan's fingers wagged in the air as he repeated Sally's insults.

"She's just jealous of your cooking," Julie reassured Marilyn. "A lot of cultures are passionate about seared fish, and I've been getting well-done steaks my whole life. I don't care how charred they are on the outside. If Sally thinks a little burned cheese makes you an amateur, then she's just jealous of you!"

"Hey, you should look at your daughter!" Caroline said to Ethan.

"No, she's fine. She can take care of herself," Ethan replied, taking another long sip.

"That Sally will eat her words . . . and my casserole too!" Marilyn fumed and took another long drink of wine.

A loud murmur erupted from the people at the picnic. Marilyn tossed back the rest of her wine and held her glass out for Ethan to refill it, ranting while he poured. "I'm so glad I got that recipe from Mom and not from Mabel! Mabel's always trying to outdo me! Sally will remember how good the casserole is when I show up at her party."

"No, seriously, your daughter!" another woman on the beach shouted, this one further away. Marilyn looked in the woman's direction for a second but mostly ignored her.

"You do agree that my wife makes a great casserole, right?" Ethan asked the people seated around him. "You should never ignore the cook."

"Yes, but your daughter; you really need to check up on

11

her more often!" This time, the comment came from one of the men at a nearby blanket, who immediately stood up to get a better view of the water.

Ethan raised his eyebrows for a second, then responded, "Yes, isn't she the most precious angel?" But the man had already begun walking away as Ethan spoke. "We don't have to do a thing to entertain her. It's the Grace of God that we have such a precious angel. So many kids these days are absolute terrors. But not our Ophelia. I've tried every day to teach her how to behave. You can learn a lot from car salesmen like me. They have the best people skills on earth."

"Oh, I know," Marilyn agreed.

"Hey, Ethan, where did your daughter take off to anyway?" Julie asked.

"Oh, I don't know, but she'll be fine," Ethan assured her. "She probably just wandered off to the hot dog cart. As I was saying, there's nothing that beats the grace of God, am I right?"

"Yes, but you should also look after your daughter!" Julie insisted.

Some of the other women on the beach had started to turn and whisper to each other. Ethan noticed the behavior but didn't think much more about it.

"I'm so glad I married someone who sees the glory of God," Marilyn said. "Men these days just want the earthly treasures. But my Ethan knows what's really important to a man or a woman."

"That's right," Ethan confirmed. "They want a nice, fancy, smooth-running car!"

"How is that important right now? Are you two crazy?!"

As Caroline spoke, she kept looking behind Marilyn and cavorting back and forth to get a better view of the scene that was unfolding in front of her.

"Well, you said you wanted to talk about how Richard doesn't treat you right, and he's not here today," Ethan continued. "So, sit down and have a chat with me. I don't know why you're so nervous all of a sudden. Is Richard on the beach right now?"

"This has nothing to do with Richard!" Caroline shouted. "For goodness' sake, look behind you! Can't you see what's going on?!"

"Look at your daughter! What's wrong with you?!" another woman on the beach shouted at Marilyn. The woman stood up and started pointing.

"No, the hot dog cart is that way," Marilyn responded, pointing away from the water. "Ethan said she's probably over there."

A nurse started running across the beach. Marilyn assumed that the nurse was running to help someone else, but to her surprise, the nurse ran over to Marilyn and started shaking her arms. "Snap out of it! Your daughter's in danger! She went underwater a minute ago, and she hasn't come back up!"

Marilyn turned around and faced the water in horror. "What?! Why didn't anyone tell me?!"

"What's your daughter's name?" the nurse asked.

"Ophelia! Her name is Ophelia!"

A man ran into the river at full speed, rushing in over his hips. He dove underwater but came up empty-handed a few seconds later. "I can't see anything in this muddy water!" he

13

shouted before diving underwater again.

"Ophelia!" shouted one of the other men on the beach. "If you can hear us, swim to our voices!" Inspired, other men also began calling out Ophelia's name from beside the water, hoping she would hear them.

Marilyn looked down at her arms and noticed that they were shaking. She dropped to her knees, folding her hands and praying as loud as she could. As she prayed, Ophelia's T-shirt and shorts floated to the surface of the water . . . with Ophelia inside of them!

The tip of Ophelia's nose poked above the water. The only other thing Marilyn could see above the muddy water was the fake red rose on the front of Ophelia's shirt. "Ophelia!" Marilyn shrieked. "Oh, my God, there she is! Ophelia! Oh, God! Please save her! Please save her! I'm so sorry! I'm so sorry!"

As everyone on the beach began to see Ophelia, broad panic and shouting broke out all over the place. The man who had been diving to try to find her swam to her at once. He fought against the current and Ophelia's weight to bring her to shore.

When Marilyn saw her daughter's purple lips, she started screaming. Even the nurse on the beach couldn't calm her down. Like attendants at a golf tournament, the concerned crowd drifted closer to the scene at the edge of the water, trying to be helpful but actually creating more danger.

Chapter 4

MARILYN SAW CAROLINE fish her cell phone out of her pocket the moment Ophelia's body floated to the surface, but she paid it no attention at the time. She caught Caroline mutter, "Neglectful parents," but she didn't know what it meant. Now, Caroline grabbed a Martian stress doll from her pocket and squeezed the daylights out of it as she loudly spoke into the phone. "I have a thirty at the Greater Branson Boat Launch right now! We've got a drowning victim! Appears to be about ten years old."

Caroline's voice shooting across the beach grabbed Marilyn's attention, and Marilyn saw three burly men getting up from the beach towels. "Seven!" Marilyn shrieked while staring at the water. "She's only seven! Oh, God, Ophelia!"

"The girl's name is Ophelia, and she's seven years old," Caroline added. "I need an ambulance here right now! We've got a thirty. I repeat, a thirty," she continued. "She must have angels on her side," Caroline muttered to herself.

More men formed a line on the beach to keep the crowd away. "Save her!" Marilyn screamed as she bawled. "Oh God, what have we done?" Pushing people out of the way, Marilyn charged forward, and Ethan was right by her side.

Firemen had arrived on scene, and Ethan and Marilyn ran

into them as they blocked the way to Ophelia. Unstable, Marilyn pushed her head into a firefighter's stomach, stubbornly trying to move him out of the way. Instead of goading her, the firefighter stood stock still, holding Marilyn at bay.

"Stay back!" one of the firemen barked at Marilyn.

"But we're her parents!" Ethan shouted. Marilyn swelled with pride as Ethan defended them.

"You'll be able to visit your daughter once we have her in the ambulance," the fireman explained.

"Let us through, you jerk!" Ethan shouted, losing his salesman cool in the heat of the crisis. "We're all she's got!"

Ethan's hysterics drove Marilyn past the brink. "Let us through, you bastards!" she shouted. "We're her parents, and we're going to take care of her!" Marilyn tried again to push the fireman out of the way.

"Well, now *we're* taking care of it!" the fireman retorted. "Do *you* have a CPR certification?"

"Of course not!" Marilyn answered.

"Well, let me explain something. When a child drowns, the only ones that can save her life are the paramedics. We're doing everything we can until they get here. I should be over there helping my brothers, but instead, I'm having to stand here and keep you away."

Lifting her head, Marilyn looked around at the now-abandoned beach behind her, then forward between the firefighters. When she saw Ophelia with a firefighter on each side—one providing breaths, the other doing chest compressions—she stopped fighting.

Resuscitation efforts continued as the ambulance paramedics started rushing down the beach from the distant parking lot. The firefighter kept pumping Ophelia's chest, with steel and determination in his eyes. But he would occasionally sit back on his ankles and catch his breath while the other firefighter pushed a deep breath of air into Ophelia's lungs.

The men from the picnic continued to keep the onlookers at bay while the paramedics surrounded Ophelia's lifeless body. The firefighters stood up and backed away from her as the paramedics converged. Four paramedics took up positions, with two on each side, while the others prepared triage equipment. One went over to massage the shoulders of the firefighter who had administered chest compressions. The other firefighter wandered over to a paramedic who offered him an oxygen mask to replenish his air.

"Ophelia, are you okay?!" one of the paramedics asked. Even though the question was shouted, not a movement came from Ophelia. Her lips were still slightly blue, but the CPR had kept her oxygenated. Her chest was engorged, and so was her stomach.

Marilyn felt helpless as the paramedic pinched Ophelia's nose and forced a deep breath of air into her lungs. Ophelia's chest rose and fell by just an inch, and a thin line of green liquid oozed from her mouth. "Continue compressions!" shouted the breath-giver, and another paramedic started compressions at once. He counted to thirty under his breath and then pulled his hands away. The first paramedic gave Ophelia another long breath.

Marilyn felt lightheaded and promptly dropped to her knees on the beach. She gazed between the pair of legs belong-

ing to the firefighter in front of her. She didn't say a word,
fearful that the firefighter would block her view again.

"God, please save her!" Ethan cried out. "Bring her back!"
The paramedic blew vital oxygen into Ophelia's mouth again
but with no reaction from Ophelia. Ethan's eyes bugged out in
panic like the stress doll. "Save her! Please!"

"We're doing everything we can, sir! Please stay calm!"
the paramedic administering breaths called out to Ethan.
"Okay, that's thirty. Hold up," he told his colleague. Another
deep exhale filled the silence on the beach.

"Come back, Ophelia!" Ethan shouted.

While the breather paused, another paramedic stole the
moment to dry Ophelia's chest with a towel. The other paramedics had managed to attach electrodes to Ophelia's chest
during the next lift, and the leader studied the readouts carefully. "One hundred joules, right now," he announced. "Clear!"
He backed away, and so did everyone else near Ophelia.

The current ran through the conductors. Ophelia arched on
the beach as the current ran through her body. Then, she collapsed back on the beach, still lifeless as the shock ended. "Ten
more compressions, and then a hundred and fifty!" the paramedic monitoring the electrodes called out. He paused while
the compressions were administered. "Okay, that's enough!
Clear!"

"She's a child! It's way too much current!" argued a pes-
simistic first responder.

"I know what I'm doing! Don't give me that kind of attitude! Clear!"

Ophelia's body rose off the sand again, like a mystic. But

she was still lifeless. "I think we lost her," one of the paramedics said. He looked fidgety as he waited for a response from his colleagues.

"We don't say that! Two hundred! Clear!"

Ophelia released the water from her lungs. The dark liquid left without a sound, building as a small mound above her mouth before pouring all around her like a fountain in a wishing well.

Marilyn focused on what each paramedic was doing as Ophelia came back to life since watching Ophelia herself was too painful. One paramedic, a younger man, was peeling the water-damaged electrodes from Ophelia's chest. Another paramedic, an older woman, checked the pulse from Ophelia's wrist. A third paramedic tended to the cut on Ophelia's forehead with a bandage, sending rivulets of blood through Ophelia's brown hair. A fourth paramedic, an older man, had very strong arms. He was taking care of the brace that Ophelia had to wear on her neck on the way to the hospital.

"*Now* will you let us help her?" Marilyn bawled, with her pleading eyes locked onto the fireman in front of her.

"They just saved her life, Marilyn! What else do you want?!" Ethan shouted at his wife.

Two of the paramedics finished pulling a stretcher through the sand. Lifting Ophelia onto the stretcher with great care for her neck brace, they raised their arms to Ethan and Marilyn in a beckoning motion. The firefighters, who had continued blocking Ethan and Marilyn this entire time, now dropped their arms and stepped out of the way. "Get in the ambulance," a paramedic instructed Ophelia's parents. "She's going to want to see you when she wakes up."

Marilyn didn't know what to feel: terror, relief, anger, or everything at once. "I'm not talking to you," Marilyn said to Ethan as she got into the back of the ambulance.

"Fine," Ethan responded. "Don't say a word, for all I care. I've already got a headache from all of this anyway."

"I can give you something for that headache," one of the paramedics said. He handed Ethan a pill. "It's just going to get worse when we turn the sirens on." Turning to the front of the ambulance, he shouted, "Rev her up!"

Ethan grabbed his forehead. But his headache was gone by the time the ambulance doors swung open again and nurses rushed forward to help roll Ophelia into the hospital. When she burst into the triage ward, the nurses grabbed her at once. Marilyn kept flailing as the nurses escorted her and Ethan to a waiting room.

"I could have told you this was going to happen," Ethan scolded Marilyn.

"Shut up, Ethan!" Marilyn sobbed. "Tell them to let me see my daughter!"

"Didn't you hear them, Marilyn? This is a hospital. We're supposed to wait out here."

"Why would they take our child?"

"It's just like he said, Mrs. Carter. You're in a hospital." A doctor had joined them. He looked calm as he spoke despite the turmoil around him.

"Oh," Marilyn said, sitting down but feeling even more confused.

"We just need to make sure that your daughter is getting

enough oxygen after that drowning. There's something called a secondary drowning that happens when the patient doesn't get enough oxygen in aftercare."

"A 'secondary drowning'?" Marilyn repeated.

"Yes, ma'am. And if she tries to talk to her loved ones, it's just going to give her less oxygen. She needs to rest, and so do you."

Marilyn settled down into her chair, finally defeated by the calm doctor. The doctor retreated into the hospital to attend to more important duties. Ethan put his arm across his wife's back, but it only left her feeling pinned and panicky again.

Chapter 5

OPHELIA WOKE UP in the hospital, relieved that the world wasn't blurred and loud anymore. She had dim memories of the paramedics working on her while she was on the beach. But the memories were firm enough that she knew where she was and what was going on.

Ethan and Marilyn stood by Ophelia's bedside, almost hovering over her. Their concerned behavior was a surprise to her because she had never seen them react to her that way before. The taut creases around their eyes were also new and worrisome, and it was enough to make Ophelia try to sit up. But a heavy weight on her face pulled her back down, and she returned to the slumped position she woke up in.

"What's going on?" Ophelia asked.

Ophelia's parents shook their heads in confusion. Marilyn's voice was clear as day but too sharp, and Ophelia wished her father had spoken first instead. "Sweetie, don't try to get up. There's an oxygen mask on your face."

For once, her mother's prattling proved useful, and Ophelia resigned herself to the slumped position. The effort of trying to sit up had taken all the strength out of her. She sucked greedily from the mask, with her tingling hands reminding her how bad she needed the oxygen. But Ophelia wanted to talk to her parents about everything she'd seen and experienced, so she lifted the mask for a second.

"Don't worry," Ophelia said. "I'm fine now." After speaking, Ophelia went back to taking in fresh oxygen from the mask.

"No, you're not fine," Ethan said. "You drowned in the river. The doctors brought you back to life."

Ophelia removed the mask again. "I was in heaven," she informed her parents. "An angel brought me back to life, not the doctors." The oxygen mask clapped back into place. Ophelia kept inhaling until her fingers tingled again.

"Did you see our Savior?" Marilyn asked, with both hands clasped to her chest. "We were praying for you the whole time."

"No, just an angel, with golden light all over." Ophelia put the mask back on right away because her forehead was tingling as though she were about to pass out. The pressure eased up at once, and her breathing relaxed.

"What did the angel say?"

"Let her rest, Marilyn," Ethan interrupted. "The doctor said—"

"I heard him!" Marilyn shouted. Her face turned rough and dangerous, and Ethan pulled back, bumping into a nurse. Marilyn turned her face back to Ophelia with a sweet, simpering love written all over it.

"She said my hands would make miracles. And she said you need to relax more," Ophelia answered. She put the mask back in place over her mouth, hiding a smile as her mother's eyes widened in surprise.

"Sweetheart, you are a miracle," said Marilyn, hugging Ophelia tightly.

"What else did the angel say?" Ethan asked. Ophelia sucked in another deep breath. Her parents' faith gave her some relief, but the talking had made her short of air. "You were dead for ten minutes yesterday," Ethan continued. "The angel must have said more than that!"

Ophelia felt stronger with each breath from the oxygen mask. But now, she felt a horrible tingle rush straight through both her hips. It was much stronger than the tingling in her hands. "Yesterday?" she asked.

"Yes. It's been almost twenty hours since you were re-vived. It's Monday already. The doctors didn't let us see you until they were sure you were going to make it."

"The Lord has blessed you with a spectacular message," Marilyn told her daughter. "When God's angels speak to us, you always have to listen. When you can talk again, please tell me everything the angel said."

Dr. Hull entered the room on his regular rounds and checked Ophelia's vitals on the monitors. An intern with a nametag that read *Eysenck* came in behind him, and Ophelia gazed in curiosity at the strange name without lifting her mask. "You're going to be fine, little girl," Dr. Hull said. Then, he turned to Ethan and Marilyn. "Her lungs are recovering, and her throat will probably be sore for a few days. So, just to be safe, we'd like to keep her a few more days for observation. You noticed how out of breath she is?"

"Yes, Dr. Hull," Ethan answered. But he made no attempt at being honest about how much they had been making her talk.

"That's the secondary drowning we talked about. If it gets too bad, she could stop breathing entirely. We don't want that to happen, do we? It might be a few days, but she needs this time to recover. You have the rest of her life to watch her grow up."

Marilyn watched Dr. Hull with wide-open eyes before answering. "If that's what you want," she said. She looked down at Ophelia at once. "Sweetheart, they're going to keep an eye on you for a couple more days, but then we'll be here to take you home, all right?"

Ophelia wanted to shake her head no, but then she saw Paivatar standing behind Marilyn, plain as day. "It's all right," Paivatar assured Ophelia. "Your mother wants to take care of you now. You can let her."

Ophelia tried to nod, but the breathing apparatus got in the way, so she raised her thumb instead. Her mother's shoulders went back to their usual perched position.

"She's in good hands, Marilyn," Ethan reminded his wife. "Let's give her some space to recover."

"But look what happened the last time we gave her space," Marilyn answered. "I'm never letting that happen again. From now on, I'm keeping an eye on Ophelia at all times."

Ophelia wanted to stay in that silent, healing place forever, but two days went by too fast. She discovered that she was strong enough to walk a circuit of the whole children's ward. It was to her great dismay because, when she finished the circuit, Dr. Hull declared her fit enough to leave the hospital.

"But I'm not ready yet," Ophelia protested.

"You just walked around the whole ward," Dr. Hull pointed out. He had treated Ophelia better over two days than her parents had ever treated her over her entire life. "You're more than ready, young lady."

"So, I don't have anything to worry about now?"

"No. You're fine. You are released from the hospital. I already signed your discharge papers and called your parents. They're on their way right now."

"But they neglected me!" Ophelia sobbed. She was desperate to remain in the hospital. "Where were they when I was drowning?"

"You haven't seen how they've been since then. They've said they're sorry a thousand times, and they don't know how to make it up to you. Forgive them, and it will do your parents a world of good."

Ophelia tried to take deep breaths, but she felt panicked and decided to sit down. Paivatar appeared again, this time behind the doctor. "It's the first step on the road to their healing," Paivatar said. "So many people need you, Ophelia. You can't hide in this hospital forever."

"I'm scared," Ophelia said out loud. "I don't know. What am I going to do?"

"I know you are," the doctor answered, not realizing that Ophelia had been addressing the angel, who had since vanished. "But don't worry. Your parents will never let anything bad happen to you again."

"You don't know them," Ophelia countered.

"Yes, I do," Dr. Hull argued. "I bought my new car from your father a few months ago. And even though I don't go to your church, I've heard about Marilyn's famous casseroles."

"Really?" Ophelia asked. But by then, her parents were there to collect her. They were bubbling over with affection and concern. Ophelia had no choice but to leave the children's ward while Paivatar beamed at her.

Chapter 6

O PHELIA SAT DOWN in the Ford Bronco that Preacher Henry used to bring all his things to church. "Isn't it nice that Preacher Henry decided to show you the life of a preacher?" Marilyn asked. "I'm even more proud of you for wanting to go along with him."

Preacher Henry sat smiling in the driver's seat, with his black suit coat obscuring his white tie and plain black shirt. Even an hour before church and despite the rising heat, Henry was already dressed for the pulpit.

Ophelia sent a winning smile to her mother. "Why not, Mother? I want to know as much about the Lord who saved me as possible." Leaving the window rolled down to cool off, Ophelia watched her house disappear into the background.

"So, your mother says you saw the Lord last Sunday. But she also said that's not even half the story. What's the rest of the story?" the preacher inquired.

"I keep telling people it was an angel," Ophelia answered as the Bronco left the neighborhood and sauntered over rolling, tree-lined hills.

"Angels serve the Lord, though, child. So, it always comes back to the Lord. This is where I get my tea. Pay no attention to those beggars outside the shop."

"But as a preacher, aren't you supposed to help the homeless?"

"Don't you start now, girl!" the preacher scolded her. "These lowlifes are not ready to hear the word of God." Henry stepped out of his Ford Bronco, and the moment the warm air hit his suit, he started to sweat. Ophelia pretended not to notice.

The half-lidded beggars, doped up on heroin, gazed at Ophelia and Preacher Henry as they walked past. When they reached the porch of the coffee shop, which had buckets of ice hanging from iron poles to keep the porch nice and chilled, someone recognized Henry. "Hey, Preacher Henry!" a local shouted. "Long time no see!"

The homeless people were shocked to realize that this man who ignored them was a preacher. They stared at each other in surprise. One threw his hands in the air but got no reaction from the preacher. Ophelia gave them all a sympathetic look, shaking her head slowly. But their rage was focused on the preacher.

Preacher Henry responded in ice-coated tines. "Yeah, long time no see. That's because you're not coming to church as much as you used to, Chad. Want to tell me about that?"

Chad laughed. "Long story, Preacher Henry. But the conclusion is that I'm coming next Sunday. I promise. Hey, you should visit Gold's Gym! I work there now."

"Buzz off," Henry replied, followed by a sarcastic cough. "I don't need to work out!"

One of the homeless people decided to stand in the preacher's way as Henry tried to head into the shop. "I don't mean to intrude, Mr. Preacher, sir, but might you at least consider bestowing something on us before ordering your own drink? Aren't you a man of God, sir?"

Father Henry kept his lips shut tight at first. But his ears, which were paler than the rest of his face, started to turn bright pink and even swell a bit from his head. Turning to Ophelia first, he spoke in quiet tones, with no trace of strain in his voice. "Let me show you what you do to people who cause problems in your life, Ophelia."

Turning to the homeless man, Henry unleashed his anger. "Who do you think you are?!" Father Henry roared. His roar was met with silence from the homeless man. "How dare you use His name in my presence!" he continued roaring. "Get away from me before I make you scatter like the cockroach you are! You're not ready to hear God's word when all you care about is drugs and money! Now scram!"

The homeless man backed away without a word. And Ophelia followed Henry to the open cash register with a waiting clerk. "Hello, Preacher Henry," the clerk greeted him. "How can I help you? Oh, hello, Ophelia!"

"You can start by doing something about all those bums out there, Shannon," Henry hissed under his breath. In the quiet shop, his whisper carried a heavy weight.

"Is there a problem?" the shop's manager inquired as he stepped out of the kitchen doorway.

"Yes, there is a problem," Preacher Henry answered. "These bums want money from me like I'm supposed to help every lowlife I run into on the way to getting my tea!"

The manager's face sank. "I know what you mean, Father," he answered. "And I sincerely apologize. You have to understand that I've asked the county about it many times, but my hands are pretty much tied. Unless they actually attack someone, there's not a whole lot I can do."

"Isn't the law supposed to protect and serve? These bums are harassing your clientele! I shouldn't have to push bums out of the way just to get a cup of tea!"

"I understand what you're saying, sir. Did they actually block you from coming inside?"

"Yes," Preacher Henry answered. "They stood in my way!"

"Well, they're not allowed to be obstructing business, so I guess I can do something about that. I'll be out front in a minute. As for the tea, I'm sorry that you had to wait, and I'm happy to put this one on the house."

Father Henry started to smile, and the red flush dissipated from his ears. "God bless you," he answered, smiling. "The Lord is happy when people do the right thing."

"Your tea, Father," Shannon said, presenting the drink to him.

"Bless you, too, Shannon," Father Henry answered. "My throat always gets dry up there on the pulpit. Kindness is one of the seven graces, you know."

"I'll be sure to visit this Sunday," Shannon said. "I've heard your sermons are awe-inspiring. And it's a pleasure to see you every time you visit our store."

"I'm sure you'll enjoy it," Father Henry asserted.

Ophelia noticed Paivatar's presence. She expected Paivatar to prompt her to heal someone with her new powers—maybe one of the homeless men. But instead, Paivatar said, "You might have the power to cure diseases, but it's impossible for any human to change a man's mind. I'm not here to prompt you to heal someone but instead to warn you away from wasting your energy trying to change Preacher Henry's mind."

Father Henry and Ophelia left the store. Henry put his nose above his steaming cup of tea and inhaled the soothing aromas. Before leaving altogether, he paused on the porch because he saw the manager coming out, and he couldn't help watching him disperse the homeless.

The manager stormed over to the homeless people and gave them a stern face. "All right, you filthy bums! I'm getting complaints that you're blocking my customers now!"

The homeless people all stared at the manager in unabashed horror. "But, sir, I was just asking for his help!" one of them protested.

"You don't have the right to get in the way!" the manager shouted back. "That preacher brings in a lot more money for this shop than you lot! Now, ship out, or I'll have you shipped out. You hear me?"

Ophelia felt a great deal of sympathy as the homeless people's sore muscles made them rise in stages, stooping and groaning. Paivatar appeared once again. "It's not time for you to begin healing people yet, child. I'll let you know when your healing powers can be put to use. Preacher Henry wouldn't let these poor souls into his church anyway."

Grinning like a schoolboy, Father Henry took a sip of his herbal tea and pushed his body back into the Bronco. "And that's what you do with people who cause trouble," he said to Ophelia. As he pulled away, Ophelia wondered how many more revelations her angelic creature had in store for her.

Chapter 7

THE CITY OF BAXTER clung to a hillside hundreds of feet above a long-fingered lake. Just beyond the edge of town, in Blue Eye Township, was a church surrounded by manicured lawns and a forest of peach trees as far as one could see. Ornamental designs hung from the church, two stories above the ground. Father Henry ruled from the pulpit with an iron fist, but he greeted everyone at the door with a smile. To Ophelia, this was just another place to worship God.

Ophelia sang along with the choir but otherwise stayed quiet, except during the Lord's Prayer, which everyone was expected to recite every Sunday. She liked the sermon that day, but it paled in comparison to her revelations from Paivatar. After the sermon, there was time reserved for the community to talk about the wonders in their life.

Ethan stood up first, right after the Amen following the sermon. Father Henry gave him a look of surprise because Ethan never spoke up. But he nodded to Ethan with approval at once.

"My daughter came back to life before my eyes," Ethan began. "She drowned in the river after church last Sunday, but God's mercy shone down on her, and with some help from the paramedics, she's standing with us today." A thunder of clap-

ping exploded inside the church as Ethan made his announce-
ment. "But . . . there's more!" he announced. "An angel said
she can work miracles now."

As soon as Ethan spoke the words, a girl in the congregation started to shake uncontrollably and foam at the mouth. The
girl's mother gasped, realizing that her daughter was having a
seizure. The woman looked to Ophelia with questioning eyes.
Paivatar appeared on a shimmering beam of white light, hovering beside the poor shaking girl.

It appeared to Ophelia that the girl's mother could not see
Paivatar. In fact, it seemed that no one in the entire church
other than her could see Paivatar—not even Father Henry. That
a preacher couldn't see an angel in his own church struck
Ophelia as odd.

For a moment, Ophelia remained planted in her chair. *I've
never healed anyone before*, she thought, terrified to say the
words out loud and embarrass herself.

"But this is what you were brought back to life for," Paivatar reminded Ophelia. "Use your gift and heal her. Her
mother will be forever grateful."

"I was brought back to restore this poor girl to health!"
Ophelia suddenly cried out in a strong, confident voice. With
strength she didn't know she had, she pressed her newfound
willpower down into her arms. Golden light surged all around
her hands in powerful auras. Silence fell over the congregation.

Ophelia approached the child. She knelt over the child as
the girl flopped around, and she grabbed the child's head with
both hands. "No, don't! She might accidentally kick you," the
mother warned.

"It's ok. I can help," Ophelia answered in a calm voice. The girl's mother calmed immediately. And complete silence filled the church as the healing took place. No one had ever seen anything like this before.

From the moment Ophelia touched the girl's head, she could feel herself sinking into the girl's neurons. Leaving her body far behind, Ophelia pushed energy into the girl's brain with her mind, navigating the brain and helping it heal. Deep below knots of neurons, Ophelia sensed the problem spot—the place that screamed for attention. She kept pushing through the neurons until she encountered the source of the seizures.

Dark knots of electricity pulsed out of the girl's brain in waves. Willing the storm to subdue, Ophelia forced healing light deep inside the girl's mind. The storms of energy driving the girl's seizures actually looked to Ophelia like thunderstorms inside her brain—balls of electric light floated around, zapping neural trees and sending them into frenzies. The healing energy from Ophelia swirled and meshed inside the girl's brain until the light from Ophelia's hands subdued the storms and healed the damaged tissue completely.

With the healing complete, Ophelia concentrated on pulling back to her body. She had the same falling sensation she had when returning to life through the fields of lavender, and the sensation actually lasted longer this time. Pulling her mind away from the girl took every ounce of her effort.

It was a strange journey, but when Ophelia opened her eyes, she was standing in front of the girl, in the same position she had left her body in. She was so grateful that it wasn't as painful a struggle as coming back from the dead. She took a deep breath and admired her handiwork before sitting down.

The girl rested motionless on the pew, with no aftershocks troubling her. The only thing moving the girl's body now was her steady breathing. In the aftermath of the seizure and the healing, the young girl had fallen asleep.

The girl's mother ran up to Ophelia. "Thank you so much!" she sobbed out. "No one's ever been able to stop her seizures before. It's a miracle!"

A huge round of applause broke out, and everyone in the church, even old Pastor Henry, seemed full of energy. Ophelia was so exhausted that she managed to fall asleep before leaving the church as well. Ethan was in stunned silence as he picked his daughter up and carried her to their car.

Chapter 8

WHEN OPHELIA WOKE UP in her room at home, her healing light was gone, but she felt illuminated from within. Resting in her bed, she saw a blinding ray of light shoot across the room from side to side, leaving as fast as it had come. She only had to wait for a second before Paivatar came through the beam and materialized in the room.

"Congratulations, little one. You did it!" Paivatar said. "I've restored your power, and some rest has restored your energy. Now, you can perform more miracles."

"Why me?" Ophelia whispered, not wanting anyone to hear her conversing with an entity they could not see.

"Because you're the Chosen One, child. You've shown that you can heal people. You're not going to waste God's gift, and you've got nothing to be insecure about."

"You make it sound like you had nothing to do with it. Weren't you the one who touched my hands and gave me this power?"

"I touched your hands, yes. But I am not the Creator. I'm just an angel. I promise to guide you every step of the way, but I am most certainly not the one who decided to give you this power. Only God makes that decision, and he never makes it without tremendous thought. Now, go out there and talk to your parents. I've been listening to them, and it sounds like they're getting worried about you. You were asleep for quite a long time—a few hours."

"You can hear them talking? Right now?" Ophelia asked with amazement.

"Just because I'm here doesn't mean I'm not other places, too. I'm watching them discuss you right now. I'm also watching Pastor Henry and several thousand other people. Now, get out there!"

Ophelia stood up, and a push on her shoulders from Paivatar propelled her out to the kitchen, where Ethan was sitting at the table. "Sit down," he said, waving to the empty chair where Marilyn always sat in the morning. Marilyn had been sitting across from Ethan, which Ophelia realized from the warmth of the chair when she sat down. "We've been talking about you."

"I know," Ophelia said. Ethan's eyes got big. But she decided not to tell him how she knew. She would rather him wonder whether she had mind-reading powers as well, just to keep him on his toes.

"The girl you healed went to the hospital after you fell asleep," Ethan informed Ophelia. "The doctors said her epilepsy is never going to come back. They ran all sorts of tests on her, but they pronounced her cured."

"Of course, Daddy," Ophelia said. "That's what the angel told me I could do. It was amazing, Daddy. I'm so happy I healed her. She won't be in pain anymore."

A tear twinkled in Ethan's eye, but the smile stayed on his face. "I'm so blessed to have a daughter like you," he said, giving Ophelia a big hug.

* * *

Ophelia was surprised when more people than usual began showing up at her church. The only time that happened, as a rule, was at Christmas and Easter. Father Henry's sermon seemed too short, but his delivery was smooth as silk, and the sweat never broke out on his brow. When the preaching was complete, the cured girl's mother stood up to report. "My daughter, Gail, is doing amazing," she announced. "She hasn't had a single seizure all week."

Choruses of "Amen" and loud clapping filled the room.

"But *my* daughter has been suffering, too!" another woman called out. "Anne hasn't been able to use her right arm for months now. We were about to give up hope."

"And I'm in pain, too!" a girl named Belle announced. "I got hit with a foul ball at softball practice last year, and my forehead still doesn't feel right!"

Ophelia bowed her head and asked Paivatar to present herself. At once, with a blinding ray of light, Paivatar stood before the congregation, close to Anne. Ophelia then saw her angel motion toward Belle as well, and then to two other people who also called out their ills to Ophelia."

"Heal Anne first, but I know you have enough power to heal everyone in this room," Ethan told his daughter. "I have faith in you, Ophelia!"

Ophelia walked closer to Anne. "You're just the first one I'm going to heal today," Ophelia informed her.

"I don't mind waiting a few minutes!" Belle said.

Preacher Henry let out a good-natured laugh. "Well, why not heal everyone then? We're done with service, and it looks like someone forgot to bring the snacks out!" Two women hustled out of their seats at the end of the pews and headed for the kitchen.

Ophelia was happy there were so many people she could heal, but she tried to pace herself so she didn't get quite so overwrought. Everything moved smoother now that she knew what she was supposed to do. Moving into Anne's mind took less time than with the others she healed, partly because Anne's brain had more localized damage. Healing the rift in the tissue took a short time, but rebuilding the neural threads took much longer. Golden light burned brilliant through every neuron as Ophelia's power brought them back to full health.

When Ophelia had finished healing Anne, she pushed backward through a thick, heavy substance like peanut butter. She didn't have the intense desire to take a nap like she did after healing the girl with epilepsy. But she did need a few deep breaths to steady herself while Anne enjoyed her arm's new freedom of movement.

"Hey, I'm going to tell my friends they were wrong about you," Anne said. "They said no little girl could ever make miracles happen. Boy, were they wrong."

Anne walked through the congregation, showing off, while Ophelia moved over to Belle. She was surprised at what she found inside Belle's mind—all the pressure seemed to point to something more serious than a softball injury. As Ophelia floated through Belle's head, she encountered brown fluid that had to be inner ear fluid but also clear cerebrospinal fluid that would most certainly alter Bell's pH and render her unable to balance.

I'm at her inner ear, Ophelia realized. *This brain fluid shouldn't be mixing with the ear fluid. That must be the cause of Belle's discomfort.*

Knowing where she had to focus her healing energy, Ophelia fed every ounce of healing light to a small channel of fluid that had invaded Belle's inner ear. Once Ophelia had pushed all of the clear liquid back into Belle's brain, the brown liquid circulated deep and heavy, and Ophelia knew it was time to ease up.

After she had been healed and Ophelia had left her head, Belle stood up and twirled around. "No dizziness at all! You're invited to our next softball game, Ophelia. In fact, you're invited to the whole season!"

More and more people who needed healing were now stepping forward toward Ophelia. Paivatar gave her a bemused smile. "I've been having the same bad dream every night for years—the same nightmare!" someone explained to Ophelia. "I can't take care of my husband or my kids. Please, can you help me?"

The nightmares had made the woman frail. Dark circles erupted beneath her eyes. Ophelia had seen her working at the grocery store before. She didn't know the woman's name, but she remembered the darkness and fear in the woman's eyes.

"Don't worry," Ophelia reassured the woman. "I can make it all go away. Just close your eyes and relax."

Ophelia felt her head warm up as she weaved around through the woman's mind. She saw the source of the nightmare, and as she watched, the nightmare played out in the woman's mind like a movie on a theater screen. Ophelia wondered how the nightmare could be so vivid, but she jumped in, ready to alter it as needed.

On the mental screen, Ophelia could see the woman watching her little boy. As the nightmare played out, she could also see a swimming pool, but no one had put any barrier between the patio and the pool. The boy opened the back door and walked onto the patio. "No! My baby!" Ophelia heard the woman scream out in real life.

In the nightmare, the mother ran right past Ophelia and out the door after her little boy. In the time it took to close the gap, the boy fell into the water. By the time the mother jumped into the pool and scooped the little boy out, he was already dead. The mother screamed and screamed beside the pool. Suddenly, the mother was back inside the house, and the child was departing for the patio again.

Ophelia had experienced nightmares before, but she had never seen anything like this—a nightmare repeated on a loop. She could see why the victim was getting no rest. Troubled that people could suffer this bad, Ophelia was determined to break the cycle and rid the woman of the nightmare.

Ophelia was able to use her imagination to create a childproof lock on the patio door, but she had to use a good deal of healing energy to build it. She didn't want to run out of time and force the mother through another cycle of the nightmare, so she worked quickly. The childproof lock glowed brightly as the hardware and software built itself. It didn't matter that Ophelia had no idea how to build circuit boards; deep within the dream matter, the intention was enough for the power to create these things for her.

By the time the little boy reached for the handle again, he couldn't open the door. The mother scooped the boy up in her arms, sobbing again. But this time, with tears of happiness.

The mental screen displaying the nightmare crackled, hissed, and then fell apart and disappeared into the soft recesses of the woman's mind. Without the terror empowering it, the nightmare had been disarmed, and Ophelia felt even more victorious from this healing than from the physical healings she had done. Full of newfound energy, Ophelia knew she had crossed a new threshold in her healing abilities. As she pondered it, she heard a hideous scream from the clouds of dream stuff that her mind was still embedded in. But the scream faded fast in the murky soup of dream stuff.

Having backed herself out of the woman's mind, Ophelia saw the woman slump into a pew. "Are you all right?" Ophelia asked.

"Oh, yes. I feel so much better! I haven't been this relaxed in months!"

By then, the excitement inside the church had built to a fever pitch. The last person didn't even bother asking for help. Instead, he just walked right up to Ophelia and, being a taller man, dropped to his knees, ready for her to heal him. Deep circles ran beneath this man's eyes, too, and Ophelia was already prepared for another nightmare. When the nightmare unfurled before Ophelia in the man's dream stuff, she saw a monstrous car accident with three different cars. It looked as though each car had seen a green light from three different sides of an intersection and had collided in the middle. It was a bizarre and catastrophic scene, and Ophelia had to let it play out a couple of times to figure out what to do.

Ophelia felt bad for making the man go through the nightmare more than once. But so many damaged bodies emerged from the wreckage that she had to be precise about her changes. Once she had made up her mind, she implanted detours—complete with roadblocks and spike strips—to keep two of the cars from colliding with each other and with the third car.

Ophelia allowed her healing light to fade away out of the man's head, drawing it inside her again. People approached her for hugs, which was unusual because, on most Sundays, it was the preacher who got all the attention after church. After the hugging was done, Ophelia started to drift off to sleep.

Ethan noticed Ophelia fading and escorted her out of the church. She managed to stay awake until she got home. But once she was in her bed, a dreamless sleep enveloped her for the next ten hours.

That night, Paivatar visited Ophelia, and Ophelia couldn't help but speak her mind. "I don't like how tired I get after I help someone," Ophelia informed Paivatar. "I fell asleep right there in the church again!"

"There's nothing wrong with you," Paivatar answered. "Healing always drains the healer. Didn't you know that?"

"Is it true that the girl is healed forever? No more seizures?"

"Thanks to your healing, the girl will never have a seizure again," Paivatar confirmed.

"The people at church don't look at me the same anymore.

I was just a sweet little girl before. But now, everyone knows who I am. Even the preacher looks at me differently now."

"Well, why *wouldn't* he? You're a miracle worker in the house of the Lord. Don't let their stares affect you. They're just jealous. That's on them, not you."

Ophelia closed her eyes and took a deep breath, finding peace with her gift and letting it rest within her. When she reopened her eyes, the angel and the glowing had vanished. She stepped out of her room, and sure enough, her parents were discussing her again. It felt strange to Ophelia because her parents had ignored her for so long, and she had grown accustomed to being ignored. But now, they couldn't stop talking about her.

"I'm worried about her," Marilyn said. "She's doing the Lord's work, but she gets so tired."

"She's just getting used to the whole thing," Ethan reassured her. "Give it time."

"Mommy?" Ophelia asked, leaving her hiding spot in the hallway and coming up to the table. Marilyn, wiping tears of worry from her face, turned to look at her daughter. "It's all right, Mommy. It's just like I told Daddy; it's a gift from the Lord. Don't worry about me."

"But you sleep for so long," Marilyn said.

"Jesus rested a lot, too, Mommy. Didn't he?" Ophelia asked.

"Yes, that's true. He was even asleep in the boat," Marilyn confirmed.

"Besides, didn't you used to be bothered when I wouldn't take naps with the other kids? I thought you'd be happy that

I'm sleeping more now."

"I'm sorry, my child. Yes, I gave you a hard time. How foolish I was! You can sleep as long as you need to. I would never stand in the way of the Lord's work."

"I don't mind the tiredness at all, Mommy. Gail, Anne, Belle, and the others are going to live normal lives now. What more could I ask for to make me feel good?" Ophelia tried to remain calm as she spoke, but this new version of her parents was rather unnerving.

"Oh, my sweet, innocent daughter," Marilyn said while pulling Ophelia in for a long hug. "You must be starving."

"Yes, actually. I'm *very* hungry." Ophelia sat at the table until she had finished eating all her food. She half-yawned a couple of times and even spaced out for a few seconds, but she ultimately came to her senses and finished eating. Once Ophelia got back to bed, the exhaustion was impossible for her to ignore, and another dreamless sleep overtook her.

Chapter 9

THE NEXT MORNING, Ophelia came downstairs for breakfast as usual. Her parents looked silently at each other. "What's going on?" she asked.

"We don't want to discourage you or anything, but we don't feel that the church should have to stay open while you heal people after services," Ethan replied. "A nice, quiet, private space would be ideal—somewhere people could go any day of the week."

"You're right," Ophelia agreed. "I need somewhere else to heal people. I was thinking about that nice lawn behind the church. No one's using it, and we'd have plenty of trees for shade all around it."

"I think that would be lovely," Marilyn chimed in. "Those peach blossoms are heavenly in the spring!"

"The car lot has plenty of extra tents used for events, but I don't think it would mind parting with one of them," Ethan offered.

"Wonderful! I want the venue to have lots of bright colors." Marilyn pressed her hands into her shoulders while grinning.

"Oh, this will be so entertaining!" Ethan added.

"I don't know about that," Ophelia cautioned. "This isn't supposed to be about entertaining people. It's about using the healing power of God to change people's lives."

"Where did you learn to talk like that?" Marilyn asked, laughing.

"Well, from Paivatar, of course!" Ophelia answered without hesitation.

"Paivatar," Marilyn repeated, still laughing. "Where did you come up with *that* name?"

"You think the angel never told me what her name was?" Ophelia asked, slightly agitated at her mother's insinuation that she had made the name up.

"Well, that is truly amazing. An angel gives you healing powers and brings you back to life, and she even takes the time to introduce herself. Ethan! Are you paying attention?"

Ethan nodded his head. "Of course, dear."

"We need to work this into the patter. Aren't you going to write that name down, dear?"

"What's a patter?" Ophelia asked.

"Oh, you know, everything announcers go on about, or the stories magicians work into their acts. That kind of stuff."

"Oh, all right."

"Well, write it down, Ethan. Would you?"

"Do you think it's a good idea to tell everyone the angel's name?" Ophelia asked.

"Nonsense, child! You always need a good backstory, don't you?"

Ethan scribbled some words down on a clipboard. When he got done scribbling, he pulled the pen away with a jerk of his arm. "Hey, I've got an idea. We need music!"

"Before the show?" Marilyn asked.

"Of course. Before the show, to keep people happy and entertained."

Ophelia stomped her foot. Her toes stung for a second, but she reserved her healing powers as instructed, not using them on herself. "Why do you keep calling it a show?" she wanted to know.

Marilyn turned to Ophelia with a bemused look on her face. She had been too busy scribbling notes of her own to even look her daughter in the eye until Ophelia stomped her foot. "Because it *is* a show, child. And please, don't you dare act like that when you're up on stage. You might be a little girl, but you don't have to act like one!"

"Listen to this," Ethan said, looking intently at the paper on his clipboard. Reading from the paper instead of looking at his family, Ethan recited, "Our daughter might be only seven years old, but she's got more gifts than anyone else in this room. The angel Paivatar gave her these awesome powers. But don't take our word for it; see for yourself. Please turn your gaze to the star of the show, Ophelia Carter!"

"It needs a lot of work, darling, but it's a nice start," Marilyn opined.

"Just mention the angel, Dad, not her name. You don't have to give everything away. Tell them it was an angel from a distant, flower-covered paradise. That will get their attention."

"I didn't ask if you liked it, child. All you have to do is use your gifts and behave yourself." Ethan snapped.

Ophelia didn't want to behave at all. But Paivatar made herself known with the bleeding shafts of golden light dripping through the room, helping Ophelia feel at ease. In spite of her misgivings, Ophelia forced her shoulders to release their tension.

"What do you think about a special chair for you to sit in, Ophelia?" Marilyn asked.

"Yes," Ophelia agreed. "Something purple, with plenty of cushions. I get so tired after my healings. It would be nice to have a regular place to sit when I'm healing people."

"I can make sure that happens," Marilyn confirmed. "You can leave the planning to us. You just prepare for the big day, all right?"

"Well, all right," Ophelia reluctantly agreed, forcing a smile. "I really do love healing people!"

"That's the spirit, young lady! Just smile and do your best work because your bad day is better than anyone else's best day! You get to heal people. Just do what you do best and let your father and me take care of the talking . . . and the business side of things, of course!"

"Well, all right," Ophelia said again. "But you have to give me a bigger allowance!"

"You'll get a bigger allowance, all right. But Missouri says you have to be fourteen years old before you can start getting paid actual money."

"I still get a bigger allowance, though, right?"

"Of course! And we'll be at every show," Ethan added. "How could we trust anyone else to collect the donations?"

"Why *wouldn't* we be there?" Marilyn pointed out. "You're our daughter, after all!"

"Hey, I've got another idea!" Ethan's face lit up as he spoke. "What about a souvenir shop?"

Ophelia tried to speak, but her mother talked right over her, cutting her off. Marilyn's arm slinked around Ethan's shoulder, and she tapped on the clipboard with her pencil. "I think the souvenir shop should go right here."

Ophelia felt alone. And had Paivatar not been nearby, she also would have felt overwhelmed. She turned around and went back to her room. But the conversation in the kitchen didn't end there. Her parents continued to scheme, ignorant of Paivatar's ability to eavesdrop.

"Ethan, just think how much money we could make!"

"I know, right? Our own daughter can heal people. Can anyone else at church say that about someone in their family?"

Marilyn took a long sip of wine and tilted her head back. Her eyes were alight with glee. "We wouldn't have to work as hard, would we?"

"Oh, I'd stop working altogether."

"Well, let's start juggling, then. We've got a lot of things to do before the big day!"

Remembering the angel's warning that she couldn't change other people's minds, Ophelia tried to make peace with the situation.

* * *

Ethan and Marilyn vanished from their house every afternoon for a week. Then, on the day before the grand opening, Ophelia's parents drove her to the church. By the time she saw the circus tent, she was already receptive to and prepared for whatever her parents had put together, and the smile on her face needed no prompting from anyone.

Red and yellow stripes chased each other around the top of

the tent. Bright yellow ribbons graced the stake lines that were holding the roof down, making them visible so no one would trip over them. Bright red walls of fabric rolled down to the ground, but some of the walls were left rolled up. In those spaces, rotating fans kept everyone cool.

Ophelia approached the tent's back entrance and looked inside. "Mother, you found the chair! It's perfect!" The purple chair sat on the stage. Beyond the chair, Ophelia saw cushioned seats for everyone in the audience. Dozens of lights hung down from ropes, none of them lit yet.

Marilyn turned around to her daughter, her eyes shining. "Try it out!" she suggested.

Ophelia sat down in the overstuffed chair. It felt like a throne against her back—uplifting and supportive at the same time. Even her calves sunk through ounces of padding. "How did you get all these lights?" Ophelia asked.

"It's a donation from the power company. And Belle's parents from the furniture company donated the chairs. Their manager picked yours out by hand."

"I'm really going to enjoy this, Mother," Ophelia said. "But the chair needs to point sideways. That way, the people I'm healing can sit across from me."

"Good point," Marilyn agreed. "I'll just grab a chair from the audience, and we'll be all set." Marilyn banged the chair legs against the grass before she yanked it away from the line of identical chairs waiting for the audience. "Now, I have to rearrange this row!" she said.

Ethan was busy laying fabric over the electric lines leading to a generator behind the tent. But when he heard Marilyn expressing her woes, he intervened. "I'll take care of it, Marilyn!" he called out. "You're doing so much as it is!"

"No, I've got it, Ethan! Keep doing what you're doing!"

Ophelia had never seen her parents fuss over helping her. In fact, she had almost never seen them fuss over anything. Part of her didn't like that they were fussing, and her first instinct was to ask them to stop. But as soon as she opened her mouth, a thought came to her and stopped her lips from moving. *I'm important to them, and they are scared they aren't going to be important to me. I should let them keep fussing.*

Ophelia closed her mouth again and watched as her parents, who had neglected her mere weeks ago, now worked for *her* instead of for the car lot and the grocery store. A few minutes later, Ethan switched on the generator, and all the lights behind the stage came on at once. Blue, green, red, and orange lights beamed down against the chair in perfect harmony. All the colors mixed into a brilliant white beam.

Ethan threw another breaker, and four old speakers burst forth with orchestral music. Ophelia found it loud and abrasive, almost like chromatic circus music but somehow worse. "Don't you like Brahms?" Marilyn asked her.

"It's . . . upbeat," Ophelia said, agreeing to the music in spite of herself.

Chapter 10

WHEN THE BIG DAY arrived, Ophelia let her mother fuss over the details of her makeup. Deep inside, she felt calm. As soon as she arrived at the tent with her parents, she could see a crowd through the tent's open flaps. Ethan was dressed in his Sunday best, and his dark blue suit clashed with his yellow car as he opened the door for Ophelia.

"I only put up a few dozen signs announcing the event," Marilyn said as she stood in awe at how many people had shown up. She straightened her large hat for the tenth time that day—something she would do again at least another thirty times before the day ended.

"I'm kind of flattered that so many people showed up," Ophelia said, looking inside the tent with less than awe. She'd been working hard to increase her powers, but dozens of people awaited her. She hoped some of them had simply accompanied the sick ones rather than needing healing themselves.

Paivatar was among the members of the audience. The angel smiled at Ophelia, and Ophelia smiled back. But the stage lights blinded the audience from seeing the exchange—it was only for the two of them, and it gave Ophelia the confidence she needed to step into the tent. The angel Paivatar would be there to help her, and everything would be okay.

Ophelia stood outside the tent, waiting. "I'm ready," she finally said.

"Stay right here until we say your name," Marilyn instructed. Marilyn and Ethan hugged Ophelia tightly, then walked into the tent to a rain of applause.

Ethan began to address the eagerly waiting crowd. "Welcome, everyone, to Ophelia's Safe Haven! But we're not the ones who deserve the applause. Oh, not at all. That honor goes to our gifted daughter, Ophelia Carter!" Ophelia walked into the tent, calm and centered, and waited for the applause to die down.

"This little girl has been blessed by the power of God!" Ethan continued. "I don't know what your friends have told you, but the truth is even better. The angel Paivatar has given Ophelia healing powers." Knowing it was her time to shine, literally and figuratively, Ophelia pushed the power out of her hands. Golden light emerged, and Ophelia immediately had the attention of everyone in the room. "Ladies and gentlemen, Ophelia Carter will now begin her healings."

The first person to approach Ophelia was a woman in a wheelchair. The old lady had her injured hip protected in all sorts of padding. Ophelia asked the woman to remove the padding before she began the healing. A man assisting the woman took care of the task in silence.

A hush fell over the audience, prompted by Ophelia leaning forward as yellow light emerged from her hands in a brilliant aura. Practiced and perfected, Ophelia delivered potent healing energy as she moved deeper into the woman's mind, down through the tissue and into the broken bone itself. Using her energy to will the bone to knit, the healing accelerated, and the old woman suddenly sat straight up in the wheelchair. Her muscles would still take time to develop, but the breaks were gone.

The woman's companion—the man who had wheeled her up—gasped in awe. And the people in the audience echoed him, then broke into loud applause. But the healing wasn't done yet. Ophelia kept mending the bone and the weakened tissue until the woman was strong and capable again. Lost inside her trance, Ophelia didn't even hear the second round of applause from the shocked audience.

This time, pulling away was easier for Ophelia since she could use the distant applause to home in on reality. When she had exited the old woman, the woman stood up out of the wheelchair and gave Ophelia a big hug. Ophelia felt exuberant, not drained. The clapping and shouting deafened her, but her utter bliss also contributed to her loss of hearing.

Before the woman could walk back to her chair, Paivatar appeared behind her and gave her a warm embrace. The woman trembled in response, though she and the audience were ignorant of the angel's presence. Ophelia sat back, content, knowing she was serving her purpose. She waited for the next person in need to step up out of the audience. Four of them tried to approach the stage at once, from different parts of the audience. A cry came from the audience: "Choose one, Healer!"

The rush of energy from the crowd was one thing, but being called Healer gave Ophelia pause. Ophelia saw Paivatar stand behind a diminutive man—one Ophelia probably would have initially overlooked. Paivatar had made her choice, and

Ophelia trusted Paivatar's guidance. "That frail man," Ophelia said firmly while gesturing for him to approach. The thin man struggled to the stage.

Ophelia knew the man was in serious trouble, and she didn't hesitate to help him onto the stage. Something about the man was different from anyone she had healed before. When he looked at her, his face seemed filled with something she could only describe as faith—an unshakable peace in spite of his frail, sickly frame.

When Ophelia saw the hopeful look on the man's face, a familiar sense of doubt returned to her mind. What if she found someone she couldn't heal? What would people say then? Every time another healed person left with a blissful smile, Ophelia prayed for the doubt to fade and be replaced by firm confidence. But deep insecurity continued to haunt her every time a new person approached for healing.

Ophelia was able to heal the frail man. And by the end of the day, relief was the only emotion left in her heart. It was relief that she was done healing people, done being in the spotlight, and done pouring out her energy. She spent her nights with Paivatar in that wonderful paradise she called home, recharging her power.

Chapter 11

OPHELIA KNEW SHE was getting famous when money started to arrive regularly. Sometimes, it was just a few dollars; other times, it was thousands. Even homeless people donated whatever coins they had. Ophelia also received and read many letters of gratitude. While Marilyn and Ethan went to the bank every day to deposit the money, Ophelia stayed at home reading the letters. Although the letters praised her healing powers over and over, it was never enough to diminish Ophelia's fears and doubts.

Ophelia's allowance went up to ten dollars a week and then twenty. Over time, she grew accustomed to the stage, and the people who became healed stared at her with devotion—something that had given her pause at first but now seemed more natural. Every time the devoted gave her that look, a palpable rush of pure energy, in all its glorious forms, came over her. It was enough to make the lights shimmer. The energy surged and fed Ophelia, warmed her, and kept her going. Slowly, she grew more resistant to her sleepiness and had more time to spend with her parents before falling asleep at night.

Ophelia's parents, however, focused most of their time on improving the tent. Over a two-week period, Marilyn bought a chair fit for a queen, bug screens for the fan doors, and glowing exit signs to bring the tent into a shipshape operation. Within another week, Marilyn had added a catering staff since Ethan had convinced his construction friends to build a permanent kitchen adjacent to the tent. Marilyn used her time to train the catering crew while the construction project was underway. Ophelia tried to focus on the healings, but when she was between healings, the mouthwatering food received most of her attention.

Each day, Ethan slipped donation forms into bright red envelopes and slipped the envelopes onto each chair before people arrived at the tent. He also erected a souvenir stand outside the tent and sold "Healing Hands" mugs at five dollars each. One week, a rainstorm came through, ruining the wooden souvenir stands. So, Ethan moved some of the chairs out of the tent and set up a new stand in the newly-open space inside. The indoor kiosk sold even more mugs than the outdoor one. With each passing week, as Ophelia performed her healings, she watched the tent improve.

After her healings one night, Ophelia's parents treated her to a ride to town, to Betty's Diner. It was not the best restaurant in Baxter, but it was not the worst either. The hamburgers were exquisite, dripping with sauce and melted cheese. Ophelia was just grateful for the time with her parents. Marilyn and Ethan kissed each other, then went back to munching away on their burgers.

"It's so nice to spend time with you and really have fun," Ophelia said.

"You're not having fun when you're healing people?" Marilyn asked.

"My hands start glowing, and I go out of my body and work my way around people's nightmares and tangled muscles. That's not my idea of fun, Mom. It's more like a job. But it's all right, isn't it? At least I'm healing people. And at least I still have time to go to a restaurant once in a while."

"Well, this is a lot of fun," Marilyn agreed. "But aren't you passionately into your healings? It sure seems that way."

"It's my passion, yes. That's why I'm able to do it five days a week. Besides, who am I to waste God's gift to me?"

Marilyn dabbed at the corners of her eyes. Ophelia took a deep breath and tried to remind herself that her mother always got emotional when she mentioned God. Ophelia always found it strange. Wasn't God supposed to make people happy? Didn't her gift bring bliss to people? Even the preachers on TV would start to cry when they were confronted with the awesome power of God and felt compelled to share their testimony. In the silence that followed, Ophelia studied her mother, searching for clues to her sadness.

Marilyn was almost done with her hamburger when she answered a call on her cell phone. "Hello? Yes, this is her mother . . . No, we're not at the tent right now . . . Yes, of course, I understand. But I'm not the one who heals people. Hang on a second." Marilyn put the phone down and looked at Ophelia. "Someone's down at the tent. They say they need you right away."

"I don't mind, Mom," Ophelia answered, keeping her disappointment hidden inside. Even though she was done eating, she wanted to enjoy more time with her family. "I'm all done."

Marilyn picked up the phone. "Stay put. We're on our way."

Chapter 12

O PHELIA'S DAYS ONLY got busier as her popularity grew. It seemed there would never be an end to people needing to be healed. There were dozens of people every day, complaining of paralyzed limbs, nightmares, going blind for no apparent reason, depression, or other ailments. They needed someone to light their way and brighten their soul.

Ophelia took care of everyone in need, but it made her feel as though she were fighting some sort of biblical plague. With all the people she was healing, in her young mind, it seemed logical to her that the injuries, illnesses, and nightmares should someday dwindle. But it seemed just the opposite. Day by day, the crowds of people in need grew bigger, and the tent seemed smaller.

Within weeks after Ophelia's tenth birthday, which ended with a surprise healing of a girl who had banged her head on the edge of a swimming pool, the tent was full beyond capacity. "What are we going to do now?" Marilyn asked. "It would be a disaster to turn people away!"

"We'll just make something bigger!" Ethan replied.

"I hope you have a plan for that."

"Oh, I've got a plan, all right."

Ethan seemed confident, but Ophelia could not imagine

what he was dreaming up. Not long after, a man with a Blue Eye Housing Council patch on his shirt drove over to present the approved plans. Ophelia was standing beside Ethan when he accepted the plans, and the massive dome on the roof in the blueprints caught her attention at once. "What are those, Daddy?" she asked, already guessing the answer.

"The designs for your new sanctuary: the real Safe Haven! Consider it a birthday present."

"You didn't have to, Daddy!" Ophelia cried out. Her father laughed and waved his hands down in a dismissive manner. Ophelia grabbed one of his hands. "Honestly, Daddy, it's way too much to ask of you! How could you ever come up with that kind of money?"

"Ophelia, do you even realize how much good fortune you bring your mother and me? She retired a year ago, and I retired not too long after we opened the tent. Now, we have enough money to expand to a real place."

"But the tent *is* a real place, Daddy. You couldn't have paid for all that just with the donations from my healings. You're not using your own money, are you?"

"Well, the people have been coming in quicker and quicker, Ophelia. And we can't keep that many people in a small tent. It's a fire hazard. Now, we've got a whole new place for you to heal, right by the water! I was just about to mark the survey lines. Do you want to come down there and mark them with me?"

The temptation of actually pacing out the edges of her new sanctuary was too much for Ophelia. All her misgivings about the new sanctuary faded into nothing. "Oh, I'd love to, Daddy!

It's just so much, though. I feel all my dreams coming true!"

Just south of the river park, Ophelia traced the boundaries of the new structure with her bare feet. Every blade of grass tickled and tingled, and the energy fed her until she was bursting with happiness. Both of her hands were filled with small round stones. "This is perfect, Daddy!" she cried out, resisting the urge to jump up and down as she continued to pace the boundary line of what would become her special place. "Just let me know when I need to turn."

"Keep going, Ophelia."

"Having the river right next door is perfect! I couldn't have picked a more natural sanctuary if I tried."

"I've been keeping track of all the letters. People have been showing up at your tent from all around the state. A few months ago, we started getting visitors from across the border in Arkansas. And last month, we even started getting a couple of folks from Illinois. We're long overdue for a permanent sanctuary. Turn that way."

Ophelia kept pacing until she'd traced a long line across the grass. Her father hadn't said stop yet, so she kept walking. Finally, he raised his hand, and Ophelia looked around at the rectangle she could envision on the grass. So far, only two sides had been traced and marked at the corners with rocks, though.

"Now, go that way," Ethan instructed. "But not as far this time. It's going to be the grand entrance. Once you get there, turn the other way and keep going. I'll tell you when to turn."

"All this is ours?" Ophelia asked. Her feet seemed to have a life of their own because, for all she could tell, she was walking on air.

"All *yours*, actually. I'm just the responsible adult buying the land and contracting the building. But all of this really belongs to you, Ophelia. I couldn't do the kind of healing you do if I lived to be a thousand."

"You're right," Ophelia acknowledged. "I thank God every single day for giving me this power!"

"That's the spirit, Ophelia. Now, stop. And turn right this time."

Ophelia dropped another rock and cut off in the new direction. After dozens of steps, Ethan still hadn't said anything, so she kept walking. "This entryway is really big!" she said.

"Yes. I need room for the souvenir stand, which is turning into a gift shop. And I also need room for a restaurant. You haven't healed anyone in the cooking business by any chance, have you?"

"Not that I know of. No one has ever told me or mentioned it in a letter. I just heal people, and they thank me and move on to live better lives. That's all it is."

"Well, I need workers for the restaurant. I'll put the word out, I guess."

Ophelia stopped walking. "God's healing light pouring through my hands is not a tourist attraction. The more you brag about my powers, the more I feel like I'm in a circus!"

"That's just how men conduct business, Ophelia. You're too young to understand. I didn't tell you to stop walking yet, did I? Keep marking that line for me. Another twenty paces, and you've got it."

Having to walk in a straight line flushed away Ophelia's

frustration and anger for the moment. By the time she looked up, after twenty paces, she had resolved to keep her cool. Smiling, she asked, "Which way, Daddy?"

"Left this time," Ethan said.

Ophelia turned, dropped another rock, and left her negative energy completely behind. A healing place couldn't have dark energy inside it, she reasoned. And she felt her anger at her father seemed immature. The showmanship brought in the money to make the Safe Haven, after all. So, she needed to be grateful for it.

Having replaced her bitterness with gratitude, Ophelia moved on. As she walked, she felt the healing power swelling all around her. It flowed like orange beams from the ground at sunset, flying all around her.

Chapter 13

OPHELIA CONTINUED HEALING people at the tent while Ethan oversaw the construction of the new, more permanent, healing sanctuary. Marilyn stayed with Ophelia in case she needed anything, but she usually drifted away before the end of the show, only returning to see Ophelia off the stage at the end. A few weeks after the new construction began, Ethan loaded everyone into the car and took off toward the park. "Is it finally ready?" Ophelia asked.

"It better be," Marilyn cut in. "I put up plenty of flyers. It's all done, right, Ethan?" She poked him in the shoulder.

"Yes, it's all done, Marilyn. The inspector approved everything yesterday, but Ophelia was busy at the tent, so I didn't want to interrupt her."

"Why didn't you tell me last night?" Marilyn asked, poking Ethan in the shoulder again. "I've been waiting so long that I would have come had a look in the moonlight!"

"I figured it would be more fun for you to see it on opening day." Ethan pulled into the new parking lot, which was already down to just three empty spaces. "Looks like we're already late!"

Ophelia felt dizzy and short of breath. It was almost too much to take in. The Safe Haven towered over her, three stories tall in the middle, with glass skylights dancing around a towering cone that made up the third story of the grand building. The stucco walls were painted bright blue, and roses of all colors climbed the side of the building. The way her mother's eyes moved, Ophelia knew that Marilyn couldn't take her eyes off the roses.

When Ethan opened the Safe Haven's door for Ophelia, people immediately recognized her. The line at the front doors started to dwindle as people moved toward her. But Ethan and Marilyn stopped them in their tracks, stretching out their arms to quell the crowd. "Easy there, folks," Ethan cautioned them. "You'll all get your turn to be with the healer after you sign up at the front desk. I'll open the door in a second, and then you can sign up one at a time like civilized people."

The crowd retreated to the glass doors, and Ethan wasted no time inviting everyone inside. Marilyn walked behind the reception desk and started handing out donation envelopes. Ophelia sneaked past the crowd and into the grand hall. Raised six feet above the audience and accessed by wide ramps, the stage was everything she'd asked for and more. She wanted to appreciate the work Ethan had completed in more detail. But as she neared the back of the stage, which was guarded in thick purple curtains, the doors to the great room opened wide, and the first guests entered the room.

Slipping out of sight, Ophelia found a large chamber in back, complete with her own private dressing room. It even had a bed. Marilyn was already there, tidying up the room. Ophelia couldn't help but chuckle. "I've just walked in the door, Mother. I haven't had a chance to make a mess yet!"

"I was just making sure everything is perfect," Marilyn responded as she arranged flowers.

Ophelia looked into the dressing room mirror, but a plain white door beside it distracted her. Opening it revealed a second dressing room, which was also furnished. Marilyn had left the lights around the mirror turned off, but the effect of the matching rooms still gave Ophelia the creeps.

"Why is there a second dressing room, Mother?"

"Oh, that's just in case you have any guests down the line."

"Why would I ever have guests when I'm the only one who can do this?" Golden light poured from Ophelia's hands as she spoke.

"You never know if another healer will appear. Sit down and let me fix you up." Ophelia obeyed, sitting down and allowing her mother to start doing her makeup. When the makeup had been applied, Ophelia approached Ethan at the front of the stage, with her mother walking proudly behind her.

"Ladies and gentlemen, thank you so much for attending the grand opening of this healing center, the Safe Haven!" The words rolled off Ethan's tongue. "Before I introduce the star of this show, I'd like to remind you that she may be merely ten years old, but she's done more to make the world a better place than any grownup I know. Would you please welcome Ophelia Carter?!" Ethan clapped his hands together, leading the applause.

Ophelia stood on stage and felt an explosion of power from the audience, triggering her anxiety. The sound of clapping became a roar, and the cries from the audience members' throats became the scream of some wild monster. "Thank you, everyone," Ophelia said as loud as she could, trying to quiet the crowd. But it just drove the audience into more of a fury. "Thank you," she said again. "The best way to respect this event would be to calm down so that I can begin the healings. Once it's quiet, I'll accept one of you at a time." A respectful silence fell over the people. "That's a lot better, thank you," Ophelia said.

"Bridget Myers?" Ethan called out. "Why don't you step up to the stage?"

A woman came forward. Ophelia sat down in her chair—still purple but now much softer—to prepare for another healing. When she raised her arms, golden light poured out from both hands, and the audience gasped. Ophelia's lucid experience of entering the building dissolved as her mind started to unravel, threading around her and stretching into the woman before she even sat down.

* * *

The Safe Haven filled with people each Sunday and Wednesday. But soon, Ophelia was back to healing patients five days a week. She enjoyed any time she could spend at home resting, but when she went to church, she would still fall fast asleep, communing with her angel instead of with God. "At least she's communing somehow," Marilyn pointed out to Ethan.

Ethan and Marilyn sold lots of merchandise from the souvenir shop at the Safe Haven. It was a small room by the entrance, and it had become so popular that the line for it often snaked across the lobby. Many days, the shop's contents dwindled by the time it closed.

Ethan knew trouble was brewing when the T-shirt racks completely emptied out within a period of only two days. Even though he jumped up and down with joy when the daily tallies soared past four and a half thousand dollars, he knew he couldn't keep up with the demand with just one silkscreen printer and a few curved stencils. "We need to find someone who can make this stuff faster," he told Marilyn that night, after the excitement over the windfall wore off.

"Well, we've got the money for that," Marilyn replied. "Let's use it." The next day, she arranged a meeting with one of Missouri's biggest advertising firms, Reed Global.

Chapter 14

"WHY ARE YOU SETTING all our merchandise out on the dinner table?" Ophelia asked her father.

"It's a showcase! Marketing agencies like the one we're meeting with like to see everything you can sell in one fancy package. Pete Reed can't wait to see your powers in action."

"Is he expensive?"

"Sure, but he's worth it. He's the best in the business," Ethan replied while making some last-minute adjustments to the clothing and mugs arranged on the table.

"We have to think big," Marilyn added. "We need all the help we can get." When the doorbell rang, Ethan and Marilyn kept moving things around, though everything looked fine to Ophelia. "That's probably him. Answer the door, Ophelia. You're the star!"

Trying without success to ignore her pounding heart, Ophelia counted her remaining steps to the door. The numbers winding down in her head calmed her. She opened the door with a calm smile.

"You must be Ophelia," said the tall man at the door before she could even welcome him inside. "I'm Pete Reed."

Ophelia tried to be gracious, but inside, she was a little awestruck. Not only did his name—Pete Reed, of Reed Global—precede him, but he also radiated "presence," which is something Ophelia always struggled with, especially on stage. "Won't you please step inside?" Ophelia insisted. "You must be baking out there in the sun." As she spoke, she wondered if she sounded foolish.

"Indeed, I am," Pete confirmed. "The forecasts were talking about a lot of clouds. They were completely wrong, as usual."

Ophelia felt a rush of energy as Pete passed her in his business suit. She sensed a strong connection with this man she'd never seen before. His presence seemed magnetic, as if she was being pulled in his direction. But it was more like her mind was pulled to him, not her body or heart. She studied Pete as he walked to the table, focusing on the way his torso shimmered with force. She wondered how he could appear to be so happy—even more flooded with the power of contentedness than her patients after their healings.

"These T-shirts and mugs look fine to me," Pete said. Ophelia's parents breathed deep sighs of relief. "So, what seems to be the problem? What do you need *me* for?"

"The problem's not the product; it's the quantity," Ethan explained. "We run out every day. I had to keep these ones stashed at home, or this table would be empty too."

"So, you have what . . . a screen printer?"

"How did you guess?"

"I only see two colors on the T-shirt: one for the name and one for the picture. And the color for the picture doesn't even look that great."

"Well, yes. We do, in fact, have a screen printer. But I only have enough time for two runs."

"Those things are from the sixties," Pete pointed out. "I've got laser printers that can print on four thousand shirts a day. Do you have any designs sitting around?"

"Just the two-color ones. But I can put the colors I really want into a pattern for you."

"I'd like to see that pattern tomorrow, if you can swing it. In the meantime, can I take a closer look at the mugs?" Pete asked. Marilyn handed him one of the stenciled mugs right away. "This is an image of two hands, right? And it looks like they're . . . glowing?"

"Wait until you see Ophelia do that in real life!" Marilyn responded. "Her hands glow like the light of the sun is buried inside them."

Pete raised an eyebrow. "Do you have any way to demonstrate?" he asked, turning his attention to Ophelia.

"I can only do it when someone needs healing. And no one here appears to be suffering," Ophelia informed him. "You'll just have to take my word for it."

Pete Reed laughed, then stopped to speak. "Well, I guess I must be in perfect health, then! But seeing is believing, young lady."

"I'm sorry," Ophelia said. "I can't waste God's power; it's completely forbidden."

"Your reputation precedes you, Ophelia. Everyone says the same thing: that you can cure things even the doctors can't fix. Someone with a gift like yours should be healing congressmen and diplomats, not your neighbors."

"Well, kindness has to start at home. I'm not doing this for fame. I'm doing it to heal people."

Pete laughed out loud again. "Jesus wasn't going for fame or glory, but look how famous *he* is now."

"Jesus only served for the one who gave him those healing powers, not for fame or glory or money or power," Ophelia pointed out.

"Why shouldn't a girl like you, with the powers of Jesus, become famous? What could compel you to hide in the Safe Haven? I'm talking about *NBC News*. I'm talking about *The Today Show*. I'm talking about BBC Four."

"Hey!" Marilyn interrupted. "I thought you were just here to speed up our production line. This is promotion stuff that you're talking about. Isn't that an extra fee?"

"You get the whole package with me, Mrs. Carter—every dime," Pete answered. "Anyone can make a product. There are thousands of manufacturers that can fill my shoes. But what I do is special. I can take anyone special and polish their special quality until the whole world knows about it. And in this case, I'm talking about your daughter!"

Marilyn's eyes glittered at the prospects. Ophelia dreaded her mother's greed, but she knew better than to speak up.

"Once someone becomes famous, fortune follows," Pete continued. "The industry usually asks for 40 percent of profits, but I've been in business so long that I don't need that kind of money. I would happily make your daughter a star for only 10 percent of the profits and nothing more than that."

"That sounds like a very generous proposal, Mr. Reed," Ethan noted.

"Why do you think it's called Reed *Global*?" Pete asked.

"It's global because I can give your daughter the world. I can have you in Hong Kong next week, performing miracles downtown in front of millions of spectators. You can be healing people in France, Russia . . . wherever you want to visit."

"Well, that sounds amazing, Mr. Reed," Marilyn said.

"I can take over the printing process for the mugs and the T-shirts," Pete continued. "But I don't need your patterns. Instead, I'll send you a designer. I can have a photographer and a designer down here by Sunday. For now, I'll leave a contract with you so you can give it a once-over before signing."

"That sounds like a plan, Mr. Reed," Marilyn agreed, unable to contain her smile.

"So, we have a deal, then?" Pete asked.

"Yes, we have a deal," Ethan confirmed. "Consider it signed."

"Yes, sir." Pete gave a quick salute, then clicked his heels as he spun and headed out the front door with confident strides.

"Why didn't anyone ask *me* about this?" Ophelia inquired. "Why do *you* get to make all the decisions?"

"Because we're taking care of the business end of this, Ophelia," Ethan explained. "You just keep making your miracles, and we'll all be happy."

Chapter 15

THE BRANSON DANCE ACADEMY held a ballet every year for the Harvest Ball. By the time Pete showed up, hundreds of people already filled the seats. "Your daughter always puts on a great show!" Tom Bradshaw shouted from a nearby seat.

"How's that taco franchise turning out for you?" Pete asked him.

"I've got stores all the way to Tennessee now, thanks to you! You're a real pal."

"Tell everyone you know about me," Pete said. "I'm always open to new pitches."

"Look, the show's starting," Tom's wife pointed out as the lights dimmed and the curtain ruffled. "Be quiet."

Pete settled back in his seat to watch the show. As Vivaldi's "Spring" began, the curtain rose, and the entire dance company was on stage at once, dancing with full power before the curtain even cleared. Pete's daughter, Kaitlin, was the star of the show. She made two special moves within the first minute. After each move, her ballet master would wave to her, and Kaitlin would bow to a round of applause.

No matter how many extra twirls Kaitlin did, she was always on tiptoe, in control, and in balance. Pete admired his daughter for working so hard. When the music reached its crescendos, the women jumped upon the men's hands and balanced high in the air over their heads. The audience went wild with each hovering pose, and when the young girls started holding fresh poses like handstands, the crowd got to its feet.

The Branson Dance Academy's dancers worked in unison to bring a blessed feeling to the building. When Kaitlin did her second handstand, everything seemed normal until her hands went limp and untangled from her partner's hands in an instant. She fell to the floor without even putting her arms in the way to brace for impact. Pete recognized the ballerina's controlled reaction to a fall, so he wasn't surprised by that. But he was surprised by the fact that she had fallen at all. When Kaitlin's body rested on the stage even after the other ballerinas had retreated, Pete knew something was very wrong.

Paramedics ran onstage from the wings before Pete could even sound the alarm. Pete's wife, Stacey, tried to head down to the stage, but Pete kept her in place. Later, he handed her tissue after tissue while they drove to the hospital until she got so frustrated with his driving that she grabbed the box of tissues for herself. "Try not to hurt anyone else on the way to the hospital," she muttered while keeping her eyes shut tight.

When Pete and Stacey arrived at the hospital, they discovered Kaitlin propped up in a hospital bed with IV tubes, a ventilator, and electrodes all over her. She was fast asleep. Though she couldn't speak or move, Pete gave her his full attention until the doctors and interns began to arrive.

A doctor quickly came over and settled Kaitlin back against her pillow, granting Pete enough time to read *Dr.*

Eysenck on his nametag before he pulled the breathing tube out of her throat. "Cough," he instructed her as he pulled. And with her airway free, Kaitlin started breathing on her own again.

"What happened to her?" Pete asked.

"I'm not going to lie to you, sir . . ."

"The name's Pete Reed. I actually do all the ads for this hospital. I'm the one who keeps patients coming through your doors. You know, 'Open the door to better health?' I invented your slogan."

Kaitlin felt proud of her father, but Dr. Eysenck seemed much less impressed. Instead of getting intimidated by Pete, like most people, he blinked his eyes rapidly and addressed Pete with the same calm he addressed all parents with. "Your daughter is seriously ill, Mr. Reed. This was not just a seizure. We ran a CAT scan while she was still unconscious, although it was just a precautionary measure. We needed to see if anything happened to her brain when she hit the mat."

"Did you find anything?" Pete asked after grinding his teeth. "If that ballet teacher managed to hurt my daughter, I don't know what I'll do!"

"The Branson Dance Academy isn't to blame, sir. Your daughter has a myoblastoma."

"A myo-what?" Pete asked, backing away from the hospital bed.

"You won't catch it, sir, if that's what you're worried about. It's a brain tumor, about the size of a chicken egg."

"Now *that* I understood," Pete said. "Keep talking like that."

"A tumor like this one will keep growing until your daughter loses her eyesight," the doctor continued. "Once it reaches that far, she'll have mere days to live."

"*Days* . . . to *live*? What are you saying? You can't operate on her?"

"Not with this kind of tumor," Dr. Eysenck confirmed. "It's far too aggressive. It grows much faster than chemotherapy can control. We can keep her comfortable and give her medicine for the seizures and the vomiting, but there's not much else we can do."

"It's windy," Kaitlin said. But no one seemed to pay her any mind. While Dr. Eysenck and Pete were still conversing, frantic beeping emerged from the monitor. Kaitlin moved her hand to her neck to block the wind. Pete put his hand nearby and looked confused, feeling no draft. Kaitlin's raised hand began to shudder.

Stacey intervened on Kaitlin's behalf. "Do something!" she shouted.

Kaitlin's eyes rolled back in her head. Stacey's hands moved down to Kaitlin's wrists, trying to help her. But in the midst of her seizure, Kaitlin tried to push the hands away. Her pushing hands then curled up to her neck as the seizure intensified. While a doctor tried to ensure Kaitlin wasn't choking on her tongue by reaching inside her chattering jaw with a rubberized pair of tongs, a nurse ushered Pete outside.

Pete went out to the hallway but refused to sit down in the waiting chairs, pacing back and forth instead. The seizure continued unabated while doctors shouted commands so scientific that Pete couldn't make heads or tails of them. When Kaitlin finally stopped shaking, the doctors started to speak in more understandable words. "Another seizure," one of them said.

"BP still above normal," a nurse stated. "What kind of time do you give her?"

"I don't know," another doctor said. "Maybe . . . a month? Maybe less?"

"What about her father? Can he enter?" The nurse who asked looked out to the hall through the glass. She was full of anxious tension.

"Of course, her father can enter," the first doctor answered.

The nurse opened the door, and Pete came in at once. Holding Kaitlin's hand with his own, he was amazed how still hers was when moments ago it had been shaking like a grasshopper's wing. "Can she hear me?" Pete asked.

"Yes. She's awake, just exhausted," the doctor said. "She can see just fine, too. She hasn't lost her optic nerve yet."

"Promise me you'll save her," Pete pleaded.

"It's going to take a miracle to save your daughter, Mr. Reed," the second doctor informed Pete.

"Then, it's a good thing I know a miracle worker," Pete said, letting go of Kaitlin's hand and disappearing from the room.

Chapter 16

PETE REED TALKED ABOUT his daughter during the entire drive back to Branson after picking up Ophelia. By the time they arrived in the busy city, Ophelia knew more about Kaitlin than probably anyone other than her parents cared to know. Ophelia wore a splendid dress and Pete a suit. They were both uncomfortable as they approached the hospital.

"It's very nice to meet you, Kaitlin," Ophelia greeted her. "I'm here to heal you."

Behind Pete, Dr. Eysenck cleared his throat. "I'd like to see this, too," he said, with a certain degree of skepticism. "It's not every day a miracle worker comes into our hospital. Even the other patients seem calmer."

"Don't get your hopes up, Doctor," Ophelia warned him. "I'd have to sleep for a week if I tried to heal everyone here at once. I can only heal so many at a time. Today, I'm here to cure Kaitlin, and that's it."

"Can I watch, too?" another doctor asked while entering the room. Ophelia read *Dr. Dodge* on his nametag.

"Yes, you're all welcome to watch me. But really, it's the angel's power at work."

"What does the angel tell you today, Ophelia?" Dr. Eysenck asked.

Ophelia stopped and listened to Paivatar. "She says that you and Dr. Dodge will be sending many patients to the Safe Haven after this."

"Blue Eye Township is a long drive, but we'll see what we can do," Dr. Dodge responded.

By the time Ophelia was ready to start, three more inquisitive doctors had wedged into the room. It was crowded, but Ophelia didn't mind at all. This gathering was far smaller than the throng that greeted her at the Safe Haven each day.

As Ophelia focused, bright golden light emerged from her hands, and then she was lost inside Kaitlin's mind. She could see Kaitlin at her home just four weeks prior, practicing her steps. In the vision, something within Kaitlin made her stumble, and she dropped to one knee, shaking. Ophelia noted that a calendar on the wall was opened to July, so she knew the problem started at least a month ago.

Diving deep inside Kaitlin's brain—deeper than the seething mess of the myoblastoma—Ophelia found the floor of the cranium, where brain matter floated above the dividing bone. Following the floor to the limbic center revealed small brown tumors in a loose congregation. Compromising the brain tissue, the congregation would continue to shoot tumors into the deep regions of Kaitlin's brain, setting her back over and over.

After whittling the small nodes out of existence, Ophelia turned to the myoblastoma spiraling out of control far above. Much bigger than the ancestor tumors, the freakish mass resisted Ophelia's golden power, feeding off the energy instead of shrinking in revulsion to it. Pushing her power to the limit, Ophelia flooded the strange growth with waves of gold, and eventually, normal brain tissue grew back. With a terrible hiss, the tumor bubbled away, and the last of the brain tissue grew back, filling in the empty space where the tumor had been.

With golden light still shining from Ophelia's hands, the doctors were gasping and pointing at the monitors. "The pressure's gone!" one of them noted. Ophelia could not react because she was still freeing her mind from the trance.

"I've never seen anyone get rid of a myoblastoma that fast!" Dr. Eysenck said in astonishment. "Even Dr. Dodge would have spent hours in the operating room trying to accomplish that."

"Is she almost done?" one of the other doctors asked. "We want to run the girl through another MRI."

"This is what she always does," Pete answered, having heard tales from Ophelia's prior healings. "Give her some time. She's just pulling her energy back in."

The glowing in Ophelia's hands stopped. She stepped away from the bed and sat down in a chair while the doctors applauded her. "I don't claim to understand how you do it," Dr. Dodge said, "but I'm glad I got to see you heal someone before my very eyes! When can I bring some of my patients down to Blue Eye?"

"You may bring them whenever you want. But please keep it under five patients at a time. Otherwise, I can burn myself out."

As a crew of curious nurses and doctors wheeled Kaitlin away, Pete and Ophelia suddenly had the room to themselves. "I don't want to leave until the doctor says she's all right," Ophelia said. "I mean, I'm sure she's fine. I just want to see the look on the doctors' faces again." Ophelia gave Pete a reassuring smile.

At a loss for things to discuss without Kaitlin in the room, awkward silence pervaded until the fleet of doctors and nurses returned. Kaitlin sat up in her hospital bed, looking healthier and more alert. Dr. Dodge read the sheet of results with his eyebrows furrowed. "We couldn't find any scarring or bleeding. Even the brain tissue that had been destroyed by the myoblastoma is back and healthy. It's like the tumor never existed!"

"You healed me," Kaitlin said to Ophelia. "Thank you!"

"It's not just a miracle; it's a medical blessing!" Dr. Dodge said. "I'm taking five people to see you next week, Ophelia." Dr. Dodge turned to his intern. "Find me the five sickest patients that have enough strength to survive a trip to Baxter," he instructed.

"Okay, since she doesn't need the chemo anymore, let's stop that IV," Dr. Eysenck directed. One of the nurses carefully extracted the needle and bandaged the vein, all in the same motion. "And her blood pressure's back to normal, so let's cancel that Lipitor too."

"I'd like to keep her monitored and pumped full of electrolytes and water for another twenty-four hours," Dr. Dodge informed Pete. "But at this point, I don't see anything that would prevent her from being able to go home tomorrow."

Pete and Stacey Reed both dropped to their knees and kissed Ophelia's hands. "We'll never forget this," Pete said.

"I won't forget it either," Ophelia responded.

"If you ever need a favor, please don't be afraid to ask," Pete added. "We owe you at least a dozen favors."

"You said you wanted a demonstration, and you got one," Ophelia said. "If I ever need a favor from you, yes, I'll ask."

Chapter 17

SEVERAL DAYS AFTER Kaitlin's healing, Pete Reed was reading to Stacey in bed at two in the morning. He never did learn that she hated being kept up late. Making matters worse, Stacey had lost a lot of sleep over Kaitlin's experience, and she was still trying to catch up. Pete's late-night reading made that harder to do.

"This stuff is really getting amazing!" Pete exclaimed.

"What's amazing?" Stacey asked, though she was not even half-interested.

"Nostradamus, Stacey! He's talking about earthquakes that start volcanoes belching fire, floods covering a lot of the world in water, and comets falling from the heavens, crashing into big things like skyscrapers. He came up with all of this hundreds of years ago, back when the tallest thing around was a church. Have you heard about any of this before?"

"No. I'm not even trying to hear about it *now*. I've been trying to ignore you," Stacey muttered.

"Well, anyway, this stuff will apparently happen pretty soon. And with what I've seen from Ophelia, I'm starting to believe it. We'd better start preparing for the end of the world. When the earthquakes start rending the ground, you're going to want to be ready. The skyscrapers won't stay there forever."

"If we're still here tomorrow, just read about it then," Stacey said mockingly. "Tonight, I want to get some sleep."

"Well, you can fall asleep if you want. But if the end of the world is coming, I'm not going down without a fight." Pete's experience with Ophelia had him believing in things he previously thought were crazy. "Have you seen those modern bunkers? Even the door is sealed so that biological weapons can't filter through."

"No wonder you have nightmares!" Stacey said. "You're going to give *me* nightmares, too, if you don't shut up and go to sleep!" She hoped her statement would get through to Pete as she shut her own light off. But Pete kept reading anyway, with his light on. "Good night," Stacey said, pulling the bed sheet over her head.

Pete turned his overhead light off but clicked on a tiny book light. He jammed the light's clip between the pages of his treasured book until he was sure it was snug. Several minutes later, a large roll of paper crinkled on the bed, tickling Stacey as it rolled across the blankets. She stuck her head out from under the sheet long enough to look at what Pete had rolled on top of her. By the time she realized it was a blueprint, it was too late for her to disappear because Pete was already talking again.

"I'm going to get the materials to build an underground bunker in our backyard," Pete announced. "I got a plan from a friend, but it doesn't make sense at all. It's not even waterproof! I don't know who made this plan, but I'm sure I can make a better one myself."

Stacey grumbled and pushed her pillow over her ears, hoping it would drown out Pete's crazy talk. But minutes later, she heard scratching. She pulled the pillow off her head and looked. Pete was scraping a carbon pencil across the paper, with his hand frantic and hyped. "What are you doing *now*?" Stacey asked. "It's almost two-thirty in the morning! Are you going to let me get any sleep at all tonight?"

"I'm drawing. Do you mind? I have to have a solid floor plan so the space in the underground bunker isn't wasted. I want to get this down before I forget."

"An underground bunker? Are you crazy?!" Stacey laughed. "How's something like that going to stand up to earthquakes? Once the earth starts shaking, your whole bunker is going to cave in!" Stacey hoped that would shut Pete up for at least a couple of minutes. She rolled over and closed her eyes, but the moment she got her eyes closed, Pete exploded into another rant.

"Of course! I'll grab a lot of those shocks out of those nearby trucks nobody uses anymore, and I'll build a framework around the bunker." Pete started furiously scribbling again. His mad scribbling continued unabated, and Stacey put the sheet back over her head.

Pete continued scribbling and talking, with his little book light still shining on the pages of his plan. The light penetrated Stacey's eyes, even under the sheets. Grunting and gritting her teeth, she pulled the sheet tighter over her head. It was nice and warm, but she still couldn't fall asleep.

A few moments later, Stacey felt a hand bumping into her hip several times. She wanted to pretend it wasn't happening. But as she removed the sheet to look, Pete was already talking to her.

"Hey," Pete said, "are you still listening? I said there's going to be lots of global floods—water covering all the countries of the world. It's already happening, Stacey! The rising water is already claiming islands in Indonesia. I thought you'd be more invested in this whole process." The scribbling returned in earnest.

"Well, if there's going to be flooding, won't the water flood the underground bunker?" Stacey pointed out.

"Not if it's watertight, honey. Of course! I'm going to think that through, too. Don't worry; I'm going to keep you and Kaitlin safe. You wait and see! It's got a big porthole on the top, which is where you climb in."

"Oh, that sounds like a lot of fun!" Stacey said sarcastically. "Now, go to sleep! Why do you always have to do things like this in the middle of the night? Can't a woman get any sleep around here? Or maybe you don't care about things like sleep. Why don't you stay up all night, then? But *I'm* going to sleep. Look at that! It's after three in the morning now! Honestly, Pete, I've had just about enough of you!"

This time, Stacey pulled the entire comforter over her head. It allowed her to get a bit more rest but not sleep—not until Pete shut off the light at four in the morning. After the light shut off, he finally seemed to settle down. And Stacey drifted off for a few hours of sleep.

Suddenly, Stacey woke up, unable to move. It wasn't obvious that it was a nightmare at first. Terror filled her because she couldn't move from side to side. Everywhere she tried to move, cold metal prevented her escape.

Stacey thought she was inside some medieval torture

chamber because of the sound of dripping water. As her eyes adjusted, she realized a tiny sliver of light was oozing in through a crack of a window. She distinguished lumps and realized that chains surrounded her body.

As Stacey tried to adjust to the horror of her situation, she heard a distant screeching. A skittering sound told her it was vermin, and the screeching quickly rose to a cacophony. In the darkness, the mice were an ocean, piling on each other's backs until the window was blotted out by their seething bodies and the light vanished entirely.

With only her senses prevailing, Stacey felt sharp claws racing across her foot. She felt warm thuds as bodies collided against bodies, shoving the mice into a pile on top of her. Despite the chains binding her, mice squeezed under the links, biting her flesh in panic before the pressure from their followers crushed their tiny rodent skulls.

Mice crawling across Stacey's arms provided new pain. Hungry teeth sank into her fingers, and her screams echoed through the chamber. With ravenous screeches, the vermin flooded across her bleeding hand, licking and biting to make more blood. Stacey's screams also attracted mice to her face, and this terror was greater than the others. Some of the mice pried into her mouth, and the invasion was revolting. She would bite them to chase them away, but when she screamed, they would sneak back into her mouth and force her to bite down again.

The vermin crawled across Stacey's eyes, and even though she couldn't see anything, she shrieked as she felt bloody eye matter roll down her cheeks. Bites covered her body, and the combined pain was greater than anything she'd ever experienced. As the vermin kept devouring her, she felt their pleasure as their claws shivered against her skin.

Stacey wondered when it would end, but the pain grew more intense as mice weighed her down inside the cage of chains. She tried to scream again, and another mouse forced into her mouth. She bit down, and it tried to break free, but she felt it slump against her tongue as it died.

Stacey tried to force the dead mouse out of her mouth, but so many other mice covered her mouth that the pressure forced the mouse deeper inside. She gagged as the dead creature was jammed down her throat by the force of the other mice above it, and she realized she was drowning in mice. Stacey tried to suck in air, but the mouse was lodged perfectly in her windpipe and cut off every last pathway to air.

Chapter 18

THE NEXT MORNING, Stacey was alone in bed, which was unusual as she typically awoke before Pete. She moaned and cursed the nightmare that had ruined her few hours of sleep. It had left her drained. And even worse, it left her with a stubborn headache that grew stronger through the morning.

Stacey got up and went to the window. She looked out her second-story bedroom to her beautiful green lawn to improve her mood. But what she saw instead was Pete stooped over in the middle of the yard, digging a small hole. Some distance away, another hole had been started as well. "What in the world do you think you're doing to my yard?!" Stacey shouted out the window at the top of her lungs.

"I'm building that underground bunker!" Pete yelled up to Stacey. "Weren't you listening last night? I told you all about it."

"No, you've gone too far this time, Pete! Yes, I heard what you said about a bunker, but it's not happening in my back-yard! Go buy a parking lot to excavate if you want. But you're not doing it to my backyard! Do you know how much money those landscapers charge? This mess had better be cleaned up by the time I get back from the hospital, you hear me?"

Stacey closed the window, expecting Pete to do as he was

told. She told herself it would all be over soon. And as she made her way to pick Kaitlin up from a morning ballet class, she greeted everyone she encountered with a hopeful smile, pushing her anger aside so that she could focus. But when she brought Kaitlin home, she heard a grinding noise behind the house.

"What's that sound, Mom?"

Stacey turned bright red. "Let's find out," she answered with gritted teeth.

Stacey discovered Pete still in her backyard. Worse still, a long trench of rich soil lay exposed in the backyard between the two holes he'd started earlier. A similar trench was beginning on the far side of the yard. Dissatisfied with the shovel, at some point during the day, Pete had switched to using Stacey's rototiller. Every swing brought him closer to the fourth and final hole.

"Dad!" Kaitlin shouted as she stood beside her mom in utter shock, hands shaking. "You've finally lost it!"

"Get inside, Kaitlin," Stacey said, attempting to maintain a calm tone. "I'm making you dinner as soon as I can, but I need to talk to your dad first."

"I don't know why you haven't kicked him out yet," Kaitlin said, turning to go inside.

"It's called marriage, child. You wouldn't understand yet," was all Stacey could get out before Kaitlin slammed the door. Marilyn mused for a moment about how even a brush with death couldn't change her daughter's attitude. But the more she thought about it, the more Kaitlin's last comment grew on her. By the time Stacey turned her attention back to Pete, she had added Kaitlin's anger to her own.

"I thought I told you to stop what you're doing and clean this mess up!" Stacey shouted. "But you're making it worse!"

Pete stood up, covered in dirt. Not only had his shirt been stained by the rich earth, but his skin had been coated with a layer of dirt. "Well, I'm . . . working on that, Stacey!" he shouted back. "I just have to get this top leveled off, and then once the roots are out of the way, it's smooth digging for another fifteen feet. Then, I lay the foundation and the first level of shocks. It's a piece of cake, honey!"

"Well, I guess I can fire our lawn service!" Stacey shouted as she walked away. "At least that will save us some money!" She turned around to look at Pete once more. "Get inside for supper, unless you want to eat out here in the grass! And you'd better shower up before you sit down at the dinner table. You look like you just crawled out of your own grave!"

"You know what you need to do instead of complaining, Stacey? You need to start making a garden. We're going to need lots of that delicious jam when we get the bunker finished. And lots of those peas, too. You can never have enough peas!"

Stacey surveyed the decimation, shaking her head. "Well, there used to be room for a garden here. But not anymore. You just tore up the whole backyard, you fool!"

"Oh, I wasn't talking about now," Pete answered. "I'm not trying to pressure you or anything. I'm just planning for our future survival, nothing major. Just wait until I build the false roof. Then, I'll cover it with dirt. Once it's covered, you can plant whatever vegetables you want."

"Great! I'll start planting spinach and broccoli tomorrow!" Stacey said sarcastically.

"No, you'll have to wait," Pete answered seriously, not picking up on his wife's sarcasm. "And I'm warning you that you'd better not grow any spinach. You know I hate spinach!"

"Oh, I'm planning nothing *but* spinach, honey! I'm already sick of these holes in my yard. I hope you plan to pay for the landscaping."

"Well, why not?!" Pete shouted. "Who do you think paid for the other landscapers? I don't want anyone to know about my bunker, but now you're causing a scene! Keep it down, would ya?"

"*You're* the one causing a scene, Pete!" Stacey hollered, not caring about the volume of her voice anymore. "You're destroying my backyard with that tiller I never even use because it's too loud!"

"Well, I did notice people staring, yes. But I don't care if they're jealous. And when the end of the world comes, guess who's going to be knocking on the hatch of the bunker?"

Stacey couldn't take anymore. "You never make any sense, Pete! Why would the bunker have a hatch?"

"How else would we get in? Besides, it's going to look like the rest of the yard when I'm finished."

"They can keep staring at you, Pete. But not me. I'm going inside to make dinner for Kaitlin. You'd better take two showers before you show up at the table."

"Oh, who's being ridiculous *now*, Stacey?"

Chapter 19

STACEY HATED THE tabloid newspapers by the front door of the grocery store. No matter which store she went to, they were at every checkout stand and sometimes even on their own display at the end of the aisle. They touted nothing but half-truths, but the premises made the maximum-size headlines hard to ignore.

Stacey tried to ignore headlines like "*Lava flows in Chile*" and "*Ten Signs the Antichrist is Alive*" as she walked past the newspapers in the store. But the headlines wormed into her subconscious, and soon, she couldn't get them out of her head, no matter how outrageous or sensational they seemed. She felt like she couldn't get the fear out of her mind, and now, the fear had become a companion—a companion that made her kidneys throb.

Pulling out her shopping list, Stacey headed for the coffee and syrup aisle, grabbing both items. But she paused and looked at the coffee with her mouth agape at prices that had gone sky high. "What's going on with the coffee prices in this store?" she asked a passing clerk as two more customers scuttled for coffee cans of their own.

"It's not just this store," the clerk answered, frantically placing new cans on the shelf. "Did you not hear the news? A big volcano blew up in Chile the other day. It was one of those supervolcanoes. Problem is, there won't be any more coffee for a while. The ash has already ruined all the coffee fields in South America. We're waiting on some other suppliers, from Europe, but it might take time to negotiate."

"Well, it's not the end of the world," Stacey said, though she wasn't actually sure. "I'll just grab some tea." The stocker nodded and kept frantically filling the shelves as fast as he could.

When Stacey reached the store's pharmacy, she was pleasantly surprised to see that the line wasn't too bad. But then, she noticed a sign saying that the store's servers were down, so no orders could be filled. A woman at the front of the line was arguing with the pharmacist. "What do you mean you can't do it today?!" the woman shouted.

"I don't know, ma'am," he said. "I'm not a technician. All I know is someone messed with the power lines. You can read, correct?"

"I can see those pills right back there. You've got lots of them."

"Susan, we have to go through a computer system because many of these prescriptions are heavily controlled. I can't just hand them out to anyone who wants them. The government likes to know when these kinds of pills change hands."

"Well, I don't want to wait another day!" Susan shouted. "I'm standing right here until you cough them up!"

Stacey had a lot of pride in her patience, but the lady at the counter was losing her mind. Big veins protruded from Susan's red forehead, and she spun back and forth as if she expected security to burst through the crowd and bring her down. "Ma'am, really, just calm down," Stacey said. "There's a Walgreen's down the street and plenty of other pharmacies in town. Just ask some of those places if their computers are up."

"I don't know how you people stay in business!" Susan shouted at the pharmacist, ignoring Stacey's suggestion. "You need better security. Who let this crazy bitch in here?" Despite the insult, Stacey stayed calm for fear of riling the lunatic woman up even more. "How can you be so calm?!" Susan shouted. "The world is coming to an end, and all you can do is stand there smirking?"

As the woman ran away from the pharmacy window, the other two people waiting in line looked at one another, suddenly realizing the futility of the situation. As they walked off to continue their shopping, Stacey's mind kept spinning. "The world is coming to an *end*?" Stacey muttered under her breath. *What in the world was that all about?* she wondered.

After using cash to pay for her groceries, Stacey drove home. Along the way, she noticed that her arms were shaking, and she had to breathe deeply to manage her growing anxiety. Strange things had been happening all day, and they were starting to unnerve her. It took her longer than usual to temper the shaking in her biceps.

When Stacey reached home, she noticed that the beams of the bunker roof had already been installed. They were six feet below the grass, and the bottom door of the hatch had been completed as well. Pete's face wore a self-satisfied grin.

"Honey, it's almost done!" Pete shouted with glee. Just one more day of work, and it's a finished project! I borrowed

Larry's backhoe, which made things go faster!"

"What did you do to my lawn? It looks like you sacrificed it to the Gods. I don't think it will ever be green again. That was years of sod building up."

"And now, it's a structure to keep us safe when the end comes," Pete said.

"You know, that's all I heard today . . . about the end of the world."

Pete jumped up and down on the roof of his new bunker. But even with his substantial size, he couldn't make the girders bend a hair. "I know!" he shouted. "Isn't it exciting? Imagine the force of one of those big lava flows coming across the lawn. No, that's a bad example. What about an earthquake? You wouldn't feel a thing down here!"

"I'm not going to make a fool of myself by signing on to this project, Pete, if that's what you're looking for."

"Don't worry; you *already* look like a fool! Stop trying to ignore the universe! Start preparing for the end of the world! It's important, Stacey. And *exciting*!"

"I don't understand, though. If the world is coming to an end, then how is the bunker going to help us?"

"The world won't be uninhabitable forever, Stacey. Nuclear winter only lasts forty years. Biological weapons would disperse after a couple of years, and you won't have to even think about looters." Stacey grimaced at the mental image.

"Floods go away so fast you will never even remember your time in the bunker," Pete continued. "And lava flows actually make really good soil after a couple of years pass— once the ash gets out of the upper atmosphere and it starts to warm up again."

"That's impressive and all, Pete. But why stay in the entertainment business if doom is staring the world in the face? Shouldn't you transition to making bunkers for all your clients?"

"Some of them already have bunkers, honey. I wish you could see the light, Stacey! I heard the neighbors talking today. A few of them are going to build their own bunkers. I inspired them! At least we don't have to worry about them knocking on the hatch, right?" Pete mimicked their neighbor Alice's voice, berating her husband in a shrill tone: "*There Pete goes, Marvin, building a bomb shelter when I can't even afford a garage!*"

Pete dropped back into his normal voice, deep and masculine but now tinged with fear. It was a deep-rooted fear that even a bomb shelter couldn't assuage. "Don't worry; our neighbors don't want to steal anything from us, I don't think. They just wish they had something this useful in the backyard."

"Well, you'd better follow through with that plan of filling this all back in," Stacey answered, still refusing to believe it was the end of the world. "And you'd better find someone to fix this grass."

"I'll just use the same landscapers that came over earlier today."

"*Landscapers* made those dents in my lawn?!"

"No, no, honey. Larry's backhoe did that. The landscapers just helped me move the girders into place. Don't worry; you'll have a garden here in no time."

Stacey watched their neighbor's screen door fly open as he walked onto his back porch. "Hey! Quit tooting your horn about that bomb shelter, Pete! What if it's one of those dirty bombs? Depleted uranium is still dangerous enough to kill everyone in Chicago, bomb shelter or not!"

"Sheets of lead and titanium go on top of these girders, Marvin! I'm just getting started! Nothing's getting through this when it's done!"

"What about a volcano? The lava wouldn't even have to get inside the bunker; it would just cook you from the outside like you were in an oven! Is that really how you want to go?!"

"Well, I don't see *you* making any effort to prepare for the end of the world, Marvin! And it's got heat vents, of course. Duh! I'm not crazy!" Pete stalked forward, covered head to toe in dirt and scrapes. "Where's *your* garden?" Pete taunted his neighbor.

"I don't have time for a garden, and neither does Alice!" Marvin shouted, a little confused by Pete's question.

"Well, you'd better start thinking about a garden. If the food supply is cut off, you're going to go hungry without a garden."

"It's true!" Stacey suddenly agreed. "A supervolcano is destroying the coffee industry as we speak. It's still erupting! For now, it's coffee. But just wait until people are fighting over water!"

"That doesn't scare me!" Marvin answered. "Alice has some folks who own an entire orchard. We'll be fine there!"

"The biological weapons will ruin the orchards," Pete informed him. "That's the first thing they'll go for, Marvin: big orchards and farms! They target the farms! They take out the food supply! Why would Alice take stock in something the enemy would want to destroy?"

"Her folks have guns at the orchard, Pete. They don't need anyone's help surviving."

"You can't protect yourself from a tree-killing gas or insect released from miles away and dispersed without a witness," Pete pointed out. "Our enemies know what they're doing, and they're not going to stop at anything!"

"Hey, now you're just trying to be funny!" Marvin continued shouting. "I've got plenty of ways to stay fed," he said, though not fully confident in his assertion.

"But you don't have a garden, do you, Marvin?" Pete asked. "Do you know what it's like when you starve, Marvin? You get thinner, and I'm sure you'd think that's fine, Marvin. But that's only fun for a little while."

"What are you talking about?" Marvin asked. "*You* need to lose weight more than I do! And besides, my doctor is always telling me that thin people live longer!"

"Well, that's if you lose weight by going on a diet. But do you know what happens when you *starve*?"

"If you're so smart, why don't you tell me?" Marvin mocked.

"Your organs break down and turn into ammonia, and the smell is overwhelming. Some people have died just from their own stench as their body falls apart. It's called ketosis—look it up! But that's not the worst part. If you can stay clean and survive the stench, then as you continue to starve, all the muscles get eaten away. That includes the diaphragm—the muscle you use to breathe. The last conscious thought you have is how much you want to breathe, but you can't. No matter how much you want that sweet air, you just . . . can't . . . breathe!"

"Hey!" Kaitlin screamed while banging on the kitchen window. "Speaking of starving, I'm starving to death in the kitchen! Why don't you get dinner started already, Mom?"

"Kaitlin! Don't talk to your mother like that!" Pete scolded her. "You should appreciate what she does for you!" His eyes brimmed with tears as he hugged Stacey emotionally, getting dirt all over her dress.

"Let go of me," Stacey demanded. But Pete ignored her pleas.

"You putting food on the table is the sweetest thing that's ever happened to me," Pete sobbed. "Don't ever stop cooking. It's the holiest trade of all. Don't let anyone tell you any different."

Stacey wiggled free from Pete. "Don't even think about touching me when you're dirty like that! Now, I have to get changed before I can make dinner, you fool!" She balled her hands into a fist, drew her elbow and arm back, and then swung the arm forward in a punching motion. Seeing the fist coming at his face, seemingly in slow motion, Pete . . .

. . . woke up in bed sweating and breathing heavily. His book light was still on, and Stacey still had the comforter drawn up over her face. From the up and down movements of the cover, Pete could tell she was sound asleep. *Another nightmare about the apocalypse*, Pete realized as he dabbed the sweat from his forehead with a tissue. "I need help," he whispered to himself. He rolled over on his side and tried to get back to sleep, thankful there was no supervolcano.

Chapter 20

D AVID COLEMAN WANDERED down a lonely street in one of the many rich neighborhoods of Bridgeport, Connecticut, guided by the light from the streetlights and the moon. It was the kind of neighborhood where people stuffed two thousand dollars in cash into their glove compartment or under the emergency brake, forgotten. This was not David's neighborhood. On his side of town, he found CDs inside people's cars, and sometimes chewing gum. But chewing gum wouldn't keep his stomach full, and CDs were hard to pawn because most people scratched them up.

David was only sixteen, and in Connecticut, people weren't allowed to get a real job until they were seventeen. It grated at him constantly that his great mind could be put to work somewhere if only time could be accelerated. As he was growing up, people singled him out for being smart. The attention made him feel ganged up on, and he didn't know how to react. He stayed out on the streets late into the night to avoid that pressure.

Sometimes, David didn't return to his mother's house until the next day. He had done it so many times that his mother's blonde hair was going white before any of the other mothers on the block. David felt disappointed and unappreciated. His brain wouldn't shut off at night. It just kept pounding with fresh ideas and new demands.

On this particular night, David spied a yellow Humvee parked halfway down the block. It sat in front of a delicately manicured front lawn and a freshly painted house, which was apparent from the stink of fresh paint cooling in the chilly night air. Just up the block from the Humvee sat a bright red Toyota Camry. The doors to the Camry were unlocked, but all David found inside the glove box was two tickets to the circus.

Once David was a good distance from the Camry, he circled back around to get a crack at the Humvee. As he walked toward it, he took a closer look at one of the tickets. It read: *One ticket to the greatest show on Earth, the Barnum and Bailey Circus, still celebrated in Bridgeport for over a hundred years!*

Both tickets were unused. They said they were for a show on "any Saturday." David slipped the tickets into his pocket, whistling as he walked, determined to make it seem like he was just out for a casual stroll. Along the way, he was careful to look for any lights on in the windows, signaling someone who might be awake and looking through their window at him.

"But what about the ones you *can't* see—the ones who turn off all the lights but are still looking at you?" a sinister-sounding voice asked. David knew the voice stemmed from his own mind, but it still unnerved him. The voice had been bothering him more and more over the previous few weeks. But with a quick snap of his shoulders, the presence he felt deteriorated.

Much to David's surprise, the Humvee featured a hatchback. This was a rare model and something most consumers weren't even aware of. Trying the hatchback, David jumped when it slid open without even a click. David could not believe his luck. This idiot just left the back door open for him! Now, he didn't have to worry about those pesky alarms. He wanted to slap his knee in delight, but he didn't want to make any sound that might give himself away, so he resisted the urge.

David liked to take these excursions completely alone so that no one else would get in trouble for his actions. He was as silent as a dead man as he slithered through the back seat of the Humvee, then into the front, where decent stuff ought to be. He rummaged through the glove box without the aid of any light. Years ago, he'd watched his moron friend use a lighter to see something inside the car he was prowling. Five minutes later, cops were stomping on the young man before dragging him to their station in handcuffs.

Even in the pitch black, there was no mistaking the shape of a gun case under David's fingers. The rugged plastic surface gave it away every time. David grabbed it instinctively and slithered back out of the hatchback without making a sound. Escaping without so much as a tap on the pavement from his running shoes, David slunk away from the Humvee. He kept walking in the same direction for as long as he could stand, determined to put as much distance as possible between himself and his victim, who might have been watching from a window the whole time.

Once David was seven or eight blocks away from the Humvee, he knew he was only a block from a park. He'd memorized the location of every park in or near Bridgeport many years ago. After entering the park, he opened the gun case slowly and was delighted to discover that the handgun actually sat inside it. He was grateful for the moonlight so that he didn't have to use his lighter to see inside the case, which was, of course, black—how predictable.

Satisfied that he had made an excellent find that night, David checked that the gun's ammo clip was full and securely in place and slid the gun into his pocket. He figured it was a good thing to keep with him, never knowing what he might run into in the middle of the night. He settled under some bushes to catch a little sleep, feeling much safer now.

Dawn came soon enough, and the bright light roused David and revealed his hiding spot. In daylight, the bushes were hardly any cover at all. David pulled the handgun out of his pocket and noticed the hollowed-out letters spelling *Glock* on the trigger guard. Opening the case, he noticed a lock and key, cleaning supplies, and a badge that made him drop the case the second he clapped his eyes on it.

The sight of the badge made David's hands begin to sweat. He shoved the gun back into the case, closed it, and threw it as far under the bushes as he could. The evidence was gone, but David felt sheepish and guilty. *Smart people don't break into a cop's car*, he thought. Other people acknowledged him as smart. But how smart could he be after the stunt he had just pulled? David Coleman stopped breaking into cars after that night, but his restless energy had to go *somewhere*.

Even without car prowling, David still felt dark and criminal. Every time a cop car drove past him on his walks, his shoulders flinched, and he'd turn his collar inside out. But he kept the Barnum and Bailey tickets. He knew that he hadn't paid the 200 dollars for the tickets, but he had kept them anyway. So, he was still a thief, even if he had gotten rid of the gun.

When the guilt of keeping the tickets had finally faded, David discovered a new urge growing inside of him. He was determined to see the Barnum and Bailey Circus for himself. The circus always took place inside a magnificent theater in downtown Bridgeport, and David had always wanted to go. But the frivolous hundred dollars had always eluded his grasp . . . until now. David was confident that if he attended the circus, his problems would melt away, if only for a few hours. And maybe the voice that bothered him would, too.

Chapter 21

W HEN HE WAS THREE blocks away from the theater, David felt the first surges of anxiety. His steps echoed between the large buildings downtown, and the steps accelerated to keep up with his heart. Eventually, the circus theater stood before him in all its glory, with the massive golden letters high above his head proclaiming *The Greatest Show on Earth*. It almost seemed as though the buildings surrounding the theater had been built for just that purpose: concealing The Greatest Show on Earth until just the right moment.

"No, you fool," uttered the voice in David's head.

"What do you mean?" David asked, confused.

"Barnum designed the sign to pop out *past* the buildings. He wanted people to see it. He was a showman, remember?"

"All right, Perkele," David said.

The voice in David's head howled at the offense of his name being spoken, and David knew the deafening sound was meant to scare him. "Don't use my name in public! I told you a thousand times. A lot of people would hurt me if they knew I was around."

David resisted the urge to name Perkele again, and he advanced to the ticket booth at the top of a long flight of steps. The steps already hosted a throng of visitors. Many were young children and teenagers being hustled through the doors by their anxious parents.

David showed his stolen ticket to the ticket agent, and the agent accepted it without a second thought, tearing the ticket in half and sliding David's half back under the window. The ticket agent wore the most ridiculous shirt David had ever seen. It had patches in dozens of colors and a jubilant pattern, as well as gold lapels encrusted on both sleeves. A magnificent bright red top hat completed the illusion, and this master of all things tickets wore bright red suspenders to match the hat. They held up the agent's nondescript black slacks.

"Front-row seat," the ticket agent said, grinning the whole time. "It's your lucky day!"

"Yes, thank you," David replied, trying to conceal his surprise. He hadn't checked the seat number before, and he could hardly believe his luck. He could already hear music being piped into the theater from some booth way in the back, positioned so that people outside would be drawn in by the exciting music.

David walked into the grand theater, where an usher showed him the way down a maze of staircases to the front row of seats. Three stories beneath the entrance level, the front row of seats stood directly in front of the massive, flat arena. A full-blown orchestra battalion was now pumping through the loudspeakers, with the hiss and crackle being the only telltale sign that the music was recorded earlier.

Looking down at his playbill, David noticed a quote on the back from Phineas Taylor Barnum. David chuckled at the name as he had always thought of him as P. T. The quote was: "Men, women, and children who cannot live on gravity alone need something to satisfy their gayer, lighter moods and hours, and he who ministers to this want is, in my opinion, in a business established by the Creator of our nature. If he worthily fulfills his mission and amuses without corrupting, he need never feel that he has lived in vain." *What a great quote*, David thought.

"Don't read too much into that," Perkele said. "Remember that you've been corrupted yourself. And I'm very good at corrupting people. So, I make no attempt to hide my vanity. Have I ever told you otherwise? I'm the most important figure in my entire realm. Everything answers to me."

A huge fanfare of horns erupted, and all the people around David started cheering. He looked around and realized that at least a hundred thousand people had packed into the theater to watch the show that day. "Ladies and gentlemen, are you ready for the greatest show on Earth?" a booming voice asked. In response, an even louder roar escaped the audience. David felt lifted by the roar's power and wanted to hear it again.

"We don't want to keep you waiting any longer!" said a man on the stage. "Here we go, the Barnum and Bailey Circus!" A huge purple contraption raised dozens of feet into the air came rolling through the curtain at the back of the arena. The contraption's wheels were hidden beneath yards of cloth, and the emcee wiggled a small joystick to steer it. As he circled the arena, huge glass balls descended from the ceiling. Inside of them, women spun around on trapeze poles. Beneath them, zebras, llamas, giraffes, elephants, and many other animals paraded out onto the floor.

Every rider pounded his or her fist into the air again and

again as they circled the arena. David could see how much energy they were using by the clouds of sweat showing through their bright spandex uniforms. Bouncing off elephants like they had been doing it all their lives, the acrobats engaged in magnificent spins, twirls, and dances like David had never seen before. It began to occur to him that every person in the circus was exuding joy.

"Yes, they're happy," Perkele said. "But what else do you see?"

More and more performers stormed the arena. Some of the performers were on motorcycles, some on horseback, and some flying from the ceiling on huge ropes and shooting back up with sparkling, fiery jetpacks.

"They're hypnotizing everyone!" Perkele shouted. "Just look around you!"

David watched the faces around him. They were rapt with attention, with eyes vacant and staring. The audience members' arms were limp and dangling. All attention was transfixed by the circus performance.

"Look how much power they have over these people," Perkele noted. "That's the kind of power *you* could have someday."

David watched the hypnotized crowd and started to wonder why the same rapture hadn't fallen over him.

"You're too smart, David," Perkele answered for him. "You see through these illusions. Barnum was an excellent showman, and some of his other quotes, like, 'There's a sucker born every minute,' make a lot more sense. There are around fifty-four babies born every minute, and at least one of them is indeed gullible. In fact, as many as thirty of them are gullible."

David had lost interest in the balls of fire being spun by the acrobats. Instead, he looked around at the hypnotized crowd again.

"You could have so much power!" Perkele asserted. "All you have to do is listen to me and do what I say!"

David tried to ignore the voice in his head, but it was making too much sense.

"You could make people do anything you want them to, David. P. T. Barnum believed in that concept, too. In fact, he always let people make their own decisions about what they saw onstage. Look at those acrobats. Can normal people move like that?"

David looked closer at the acrobats. Their elbows bent backward without snapping, allowing them to flow through hoops. Their shoulders dislocated and popped back into place without a problem. One woman was adept at standing on her hands and dropping her legs in front of her head. Once her feet had reached her neck, she would pull back out of her hoop and stand on the pedestal again. This was met with thunderous applause.

"She's cheating," Perkele suggested. "Sure, she can bend her body in amazing ways. But look closer, David! Can you see that line running up to the rafters? It's a safety line in case she loses her balance. She's just faking."

David studied the acrobat closer. The guy line was indeed visible, and he even caught the acrobat pushing her weight back to the center, relying on the wire to keep from falling over completely. Even as a professional, she couldn't help making

113

mistakes. "But they aren't *all* faking, are they?"

"You can believe whatever you want to believe, David. But I know better than you." Perkele snorted. "They're all faking."

Acrobats spun in every direction across all three rings. It was too much for one pair of eyes to take in. David saw some people staring at the left end of the circus and other people right next to them at the right end of it.

"Just look at all of them!" Perkele said with glee. "Look at all these people you could corrupt. Just think about it, David! You could have every single one of them under your control. That's what I'm offering you."

David thought about it but said nothing. All his life, people had tried to control him. His mother tried to control him, always bugging him to go to school, not to stay out so late, and on and on. Police officers treated him like a criminal and demanded to know what he was doing wandering the streets at night, like there was anything out of the ordinary about that when you had nothing but streets for dozens of miles in every direction. Teachers tried to keep him in school with detention, but he learned how to pass tests so he wouldn't end up there.

"Now, *you* get to control other people, David!" Perkele continued. "Take charge of your life! When you get into college, I want to see you taking control of other people. It's kind of like this circus. Everyone at school is wrapped up in their homework, and you can just nudge on in and get control of them."

"What's your secret?" David asked aloud during a deafening audience roar that even made the lions shrink in fear.

"Fear," Perkele answered. The long pause following that

word drew David into a tormenting terror. His legs prickled, and he suddenly felt very self-conscious. "I give people nightmares," Perkele finally continued. "In these nightmares, they are terrified. I feed off that fear, and in return, I reward my victims."

"Reward them how?" David asked. The music went directly to a new song without even a pause, and the new song brought out jugglers by the dozen.

"Fear makes people do crazy things. These things make them feel like they're powerful. But in the end, they always hurt themselves. It's a rush for them to do something dangerous. People *want* to do dangerous things. I just give them the justification to do so. When one of my victims robs a bank, their fear gets magnified a thousand-fold in every person that sees the robber's weapon. When one of my victims defrauds a customer, they get a rush out of screwing them over, and the customer feels insecure and afraid after having been taken."

The circus continued unabated, but the loudspeakers hit a lull in the music that was just long enough for the announcer to give one last shout. "Ladies and gentlemen, the grand finale of the greatest show on Earth!" Every single acrobat, juggler, and spinning trapeze artist came to the stage at once, and there was barely room for the announcer. When the elephants stood on each other's backs from one end to the other, people's heads were turning this way and that, trying to take in the magnificent spectacle.

"Those are wild animals, David," Perkele pointed out. "Don't forget that. They are just like the stupid people in the audience, trained to obey authority, trained to obey fear, and trained to be meek. But have you seen them in the wild, David? Even the babies are fearless. They will stampede right through a whole pride of lions without even thinking twice because no other animal is bigger than the elephant. The elephant knows that it is the biggest animal in the jungle, and it uses that fact to destroy anything that tries to stand in its way. Just because they stand on each other's backs doesn't mean they aren't itching for the first chance to make a break for it and trample the audience to death. That's why the trainers are on the stage at the same time."

The elephants concluded their performance, and once they cleared from the stage, a group of horses followed suit, and then llamas, and then the performers again. The last one to leave the stage was a goofy clown. He had been busy playing with a flower on an acrobat's dress, and it came off in his hand. He was too fascinated with the flower to see the circus leave. His massive boots flapping around and his arms flailing through the air as he left the stage made the audience howl with laughter.

The lights came up, and everyone started standing at once and making their way through the exits. It seemed to David like everyone had been hypnotized to the point of pacifism because no fighting broke out as hordes of children and parents filed through the wide arena exits. Even as the crowd dispersed across the parking lots and busy streets, the people remained relatively passive and calm. David disappeared into the city with them.

Within minutes, David was just another passerby—a random citizen wandering the streets. Deep inside, David knew that he was destined for greatness, and he dreamed of the thousands of people he would control. No, better make that millions. David had plans to control as many people as he possibly could. He knew he had the best teacher and that his teacher could control his victims' minds with mind-ripping fear.

Chapter 22

BEFORE DAVID KNEW IT, high school ended, and college started. He began a major in biology. It was a major that would allow him access to the most innocent professions he could conceive of, he figured. Some people laughed at him when he told them he wanted to be a biologist. Perkele mocked him, too. "What, you're just going to study frogs all day?" Perkele asked.

David smiled, knowing that no one, even Perkele, could suspect the real reason he wanted to be in biology classes: dissections. David loved having the chance to tear another creature apart. Okay, maybe it wasn't alive anymore. But that didn't make it any less exciting. When David had taken apart a pigeon as a little boy, his mother had slapped him and told him to have respect for the dead. This confused David. He had respect for the animal, didn't he? All he wanted to do was see why the animal died and how it worked on the inside. So, he had pulled it apart out of curiosity.

David was surprised to discover that his college had less security than his high school. And even the security guards who did patrol the campus had classes of their own to go to, so they were kept busy. Nevertheless, David seemed to get at least one hand wave from a security guard every time he walked to class.

By the time David made it to class every day, he was always edgy. Biology lectures got boring, but his anxiety kept him awake through every class. The fun began in lab classes, where dissections took place. David loved the cold, sterile flavor of the formaldehyde in the air, evaporating from the buckets placed by each table. One week, it would be baby pigs in the buckets, and the next week, frogs.

David's fingers were deft and sensitive. Throughout his life, people had made fun of his delicate hands and called him names like "piano fingers." In biology class, though, people seemed jealous of his delicate hands. When his fingers were preoccupied peeling open a pig belly from end to end, they had no time to follow the urge to pick a lock or slide open a desk drawer when no one was looking.

Other students stared at David from time to time as he performed a task like flawlessly separating a pig's trachea. The scalpel went right between the neck tissue and the voice box, leaving the neck veins connected and flawless, shining blue in the cavity left by the voice box. He knew it was a thing of wonder to behold, and the excellent grades he achieved made up for all the time he had spent in detention in high school. At last, his genius was being recognized.

Inside the tiny, peeled corpses, David found illumination. Delicate, miniature organs lay inside, perfectly still, arranged like a jigsaw puzzle. Surely, the Maker had a plan when he built these perfect bodies.

Extracting the pig's spleen, gallbladder, and pancreas with precision, David marked the cavities with tiny blue flags like he did for every assignment. Then, he peeled back the intestines to extract the kidneys and mark the indents with yellow flags. When he was done with the dissection, he took a step back and admired his handiwork.

Suddenly, the pig's face transformed in front of David. The security guard he'd seen on the way to class lay on the table before him. His face was twisted in pain, and his tiny lungs fluttered inside the exposed ribcage. "Look what you've done to me!" screamed the dissected security guard.

"No!" David shouted in horror while waving his scalpel. But then, the pig was back on the table, looking still and serene. The piglet's face—the only thing untouched by David's scalpel—rested in peace.

"Are you all right, Mr. Coleman?" David's professor asked.

David looked at the teacher and realized his mistake. "Um . . . yes! I thought I . . . saw a fly," he stuttered out. "I didn't want it getting near the specimen. I'm finished marking all the organs, by the way."

"Very good, David," the professor responded. Stepping over to the dissection table, the professor gave David a thumbs-up. "You're going to be a great scientist someday. This is the first 100 I'm giving out this week, ladies and gentlemen. A perfect score."

David's cheeks flushed. He gave a small nod and smiled as the other students clapped. But David's hands never stopped gripping the edge of the table, and the students never saw the small cuts on his bottom lip where he bit down in anxiety.

Chapter 23

A FOUL MOOD FOLLOWED David back to his dorm. He closed the dorm's outer door as fast as he could, even though he knew another guy was right behind him. He proceeded to his room.

The college had stuck David in a room with a foul-smelling creature named Richard, who lounged on his bed drinking beer when he wasn't in class. David knew Richard had been skipping some classes that day because Richard's eyes were glassed over and his breath was rotten. "Mrs. Fisher's class got canceled again," Richard claimed. "She's still got the flu."

"No, she doesn't," David responded. "I saw Mrs. Fisher teaching CPR class today. She's not sick."

"Hey, I noticed that thing you wrote in your notebook, man. You know: 'If you can't control something, own it.' What in the world does that mean?"

"You looked at my notebook?" David growled.

Even with glassed-over eyes, Richard seemed dangerous and dominating as he sat up straight in bed. The fact that he was also rocking back and forth made him look like a spitting cobra, ready to lurch forward on his alcoholic engine and strike without warning. "Easy now, man," he said. "It's just a notebook. It's not like it's your diary or something. And it's not like I was stealing your homework or anything."

David maintained his composure. But inside, he was ready to sting back if he had to. "Look, Richard, it's my personal stuff, okay? That's something my father always used to say to me when I was a child. I can't believe I have to say it to someone *your* age."

Richard scratched his head. It didn't look to David like Richard was thinking, though. It looked more like he had mange or something. "No, that doesn't make sense," Richard finally said, burping as the phrase came out.

"Oh, don't be stupid, Richard." David stayed completely still and calm as he spoke. But there was a darkness about him that was enough to silence the fool sitting on the bed across from him. "Why in the world did they make these rooms so small? Anyway . . . what my father was talking about, and what you'll never understand is this: you've got to give people what they ask of you—what they want."

Richard said nothing in his defense. He just sat there scratching his head again as David paused for breath.

"Once you give someone what they really want, that's when they start to feel freedom," David continued. "And when they feel that freedom, they start to feel powerful and in control. But with *you* having the ability to give them what they want or not, it's really *you* who is in control. You've got the person right in the palm of your hand. People with weak minds are easy to take over, Richard."

"I don't understand what you're on about at all," Richard responded. He let out another belch.

"Right. You just don't get it," David agreed. "You never

will." David yanked his notebook off Richard's bed and tucked it away with the rest of his schoolwork. Then, he pulled out his anatomy textbook and buried himself in the text.

"So, that's it?" Richard asked. "You're just going to ignore me now?"

David reluctantly looked up again. "Pretty much. You're just my roommate at this point. Nothing more," he said. "But if I want to control you, believe me, I'll do it." David returned his attention to the anatomy text as he heard the hiss of another beer bottle opening.

After a while, David put his textbook away and headed downstairs for food. It was a short walk to the cafeteria, and once he sat down to eat, he zeroed in on a nice-looking young freshman girl eating all by herself. She was stirring her peas around with her fork like she was making sand art rather than eating lunch.

Deep inside David's mind, a dark voice spoke up. "You need to get GHB, boy. Three drops of that stuff, and you'll be riding that racehorse in no time flat." David felt his face turn red, and he tried his best to focus on his meal of tamales. He felt ashamed.

After a few moments, the voice returned. "I'm sure those drunks in your hall have some roofies hidden somewhere, don't they? Dig around in their drawers to find it."

David tried his best to ignore the voice. He stared deep into his plate of tamales. But the voice would not leave him. "You know you want to do it," the voice continued. David started chewing with vigor. "Go on, David. It will make you feel powerful."

David angrily bit into a tamale. "That's it, David, get mad!" Perkele was relentless. He'd stayed harmless in the background of David's mind for a long time. But now, he was back in full force. David dropped the rest of the tamale on the plate. He couldn't wait to get away from the table. "What's wrong? Are you chickening out on me?" Perkele needled him.

David stood up and headed off to the tray return, trying to get away as fast as he could. He didn't want to talk back to the voice—not when he was in public. Once he got into a stairwell, he found it unoccupied. "Leave me alone!" he shouted at Perkele.

David ran up the stairs. Reaching the third floor of the dorm, he exited to the hallway and made it to his room. He sighed in deep relief when he saw that Richard was not there.

"If you think I'm going to leave you alone, you can forget about it," Perkele continued. David threw himself on his bed and covered his ears with his hands. But the voice kept on him, un-muffled. "Get off your lazy bum and go control someone!" it said.

"No!" David responded.

"Yes! Get looking. Now!"

David pounded his bed with his fists in frustration. "Go away, Perkele!"

"No. We're not *ever* going away!"

"What do you mean, 'we'?" David asked.

"I'm here, too," a darker voice responded. "And I'm not going anywhere either. You'd better start liking me because I certainly don't like you very much so far."

"Well, I don't like you either!" David shouted.

The dark voice was quiet for a few moments. But then, it returned. "Perkele is serious, you know."

"What do you mean?"

"Go through Richard's stuff!" the voice demanded.

"No!" David asserted. "I don't steal anymore. Not since the incident with the gun." David had tried to repress the memory, but it flooded back to him. A few days after he had stolen the gun, he read in the paper that a retired officer had been murdered during a home invasion. The story mentioned that the cop's gun was missing.

"Right! You already killed a cop. So, a simple rape is nothing compared to that. Get going and be a man!" This new sinister voice was as relentless as Perkele.

"No, no, no. No!" David repeated as he continued to lay face-down on the bed. "I'm not listening to you or Perkele anymore!" David shot back. "I'm going to lie here until you both go away!"

"Don't you get it, David? We're not leaving." David rolled over and stared at the ceiling, trying to ignore the voice.

"You're really just going to stare at the ceiling all day?" Perkele's voice chimed back in. "Don't you have classes to go to?"

"Yes," David replied. "And you two clowns are going to stay here while I go to them!" David remained on the bed, though.

"Well, shouldn't you get going?"

"I can wait another ten minutes and still get there on time," David pointed out.

"Fine, then I'll just watch you. But you're still a chicken!"

David's head was filled with awful imitations of screech-ing chickens for the next ten minutes while he stayed rooted to his bed. When it was time for him to leave for class, he rose off the bed and left the room with his backpack. As his feet pound-ed in the corridor, the troublesome voices didn't seem to follow him.

By the time David reached his class, a dull headache threatened to keep him from concentrating. There was a test that day, and David knew he was missing some answers, but he was too frustrated about Perkele's return to care. For the time being, he basked in the silence the voices were affording him.

When he finished his test, David felt exhausted and sick. As he dropped his test off at the front of the room, he passed the animal skulls displayed on his professor's desk. As David dropped his test in the collection box, he swore he saw one of the skulls hop into the air for a moment before dropping back to the desk. He stared at the offending skull, but it stayed motionless. As he turned and walked away, he heard a thud on the table that was the exact sound the skull had made when it landed.

David ran from the classroom as fast as he could. But the thudding sounds seemed to chase him out of the classroom, following close behind. He was sure the skulls were following him, but he refused to turn and confirm it. He tore down the campus's walkways, taking a different route than usual back to the dorm, hoping to lose the skulls.

No matter how fast or far David ran, he couldn't escape what was now crazy laughter in his head. He knew that the three high-pitched laughing voices he was hearing came from the skulls. Their voices joined in with the two voices from before. And by the time David returned to his dorm room, there was so much chaos in his head that he couldn't focus on anything else. David flopped on the bed and covered his ears again.

The voices stopped, and David raised his head. Looking at his cell phone, he saw that the time had advanced several hours, and morning sunlight surrounded him. He still had all his clothes on from the night before, but he couldn't find any trace of his backpack. Looking around, David realized that he was in the wheat fields beyond campus. He figured he was a good five or six miles from his dorm.

As David stood up, he discovered strange clumps of what looked to be matted black hair clinging to his pants. He frantically ripped at the clumps, trying to pull them off. And as he did so, he realized that the hair was glued to his pants with dry skin and blood. But the clumps were too bloody and matted for him to tell whether the hair and skin were from an animal or . . . No, David couldn't even bring himself to think of the other possibility.

The voices were gone for the moment. And Richard was, too. David had received some strange stares from passing students on his way back to his dorm. But nobody bothered to question him about his appearance.

Chapter 24

BACK IN HIS dorm room, David found his backpack under his bed. He felt relieved and started to relax. At least he had been smart enough to leave his backpack somewhere safe. But he couldn't figure out what made him black out. The voices had always bothered him, but they had never made him pass out. He started to wonder if he had been drugged.

David showered, changed into clean clothes, and left his room before any chaos could begin in his head. Downstairs, in the dorm's lounge, he saw some of his fellow students watching *The Kathryn Cornich Show* on TV. Cornich was interviewing a healer from Missouri. The girls watching didn't take their eyes off the TV for even a moment when David came in. He had resigned himself to being treated like he didn't exist a long time ago.

A stunning young woman sat across from Kathryn Cornich, looking demure and almost vulnerable in the studio lights. A banner at the bottom of the screen identified her as the guest: *Ophelia Carter, Gifted Healer*. Cornich scratched her head as she posed the first question. "So, Ophelia, I cannot believe this. You were only seven years old when you started healing people?"

"That's correct," Ophelia confirmed, smiling. "I've been healing people for most of my life. It's a gift I never want to part with."

A loud burst of applause paused the conversation. Cornich waited for the applause to die down before continuing. "Your father is in the audience today, as well as your mother. Would you please stand up, Ethan and Marilyn?"

The TV switched to a view of the audience, with the camera trained on Ethan and Marilyn as they stood. Toward the bottom of the screen, a banner said: *Proud Parents, Ethan and Marilyn Carter.* David committed their names to memory.

"I knew they would be here today," Ophelia said. "They've always been my biggest supporters." As Ethan and Marilyn smiled, nodded, and waved in acknowledgment of the attention, the TV switched back to the shot of Cornich and Ophelia.

"Could we have a map?" Cornich asked. Within seconds, a map of Missouri appeared on the screen. "Let's zoom in," Cornich said, and a pop-up map of Blue Eye Township appeared. A marker identified the location of the Safe Haven. "Wouldn't Branson a better place to do healings? It's larger than Blue Eye, and more tourists drive through there."

"Yes, I know all about Branson, Kathryn," Ophelia responded. She was now a confident young woman. "But the attention's not what I'm after. I'm looking for the troubled minds and tortured souls—the ones who my healing hands can help. One way I can tell they truly need me is if they're willing to travel further than Branson, to Blue Eye."

"Well, speaking of that, we've assembled some people in need today," Cornich informed Ophelia. "They're right here in the studio audience. Are you able to demonstrate your powers for us today? I would like to see it for myself."

"I prefer to do the healings at the Safe Haven," Ophelia responded. "As I mentioned, I'm not out for attention. But yes, I suppose I can try to focus enough for one healing. I've got my hands here with me, don't I?"

An audience member put his arm into the air, and Cornich pointed him out to Ophelia. The man's arm was shaking as it remained stretched above his head. "That man needs healing more than anyone else," Cornich explained.

"Consider it done," Ophelia said. She walked into the audience and toward the man.

Cornich was too excited to remain seated, and she strode to the edge of the stage to get a better view. As the studio lights focused on the man, Ophelia stood among the audience members and healed him right there in his seat. The reactions on the audience members' faces ranged from disbelief to absolute exultation as they witnessed the healing. But the bright yellow light from Ophelia's hands was apparently too much for the video feed to handle. To the viewing audience at home, shimmering pixels demonstrated the intensity of the healing, if not the actual color of the brilliant light emanating from Ophelia.

When the light had faded from view, the man opened his eyes, which contained tears that shimmered in the studio lights. The man hugged Ophelia with all his might. A student named Molly, watching from the dorm's lounge, made all the decisions in her group of friends. "I'm talking to the student council this weekend," she declared. "I want this woman to attend our college!"

Molly's friends always agreed with everything she said. "I want her to come here, too," one of them said. "Me, too," another agreed. The other girls around Molly simply nodded their heads in approval.

As David went to his classes that day, he couldn't stop thinking about Ophelia Carter, either. He wondered if this amazing healer might be able to take away the voices in his head. He brimmed with newfound confidence at the thought while also brimming with anger at the voices.

"You hear that?" Perkele said to the other voice. "This little bugger is trying to get rid of us!"

"Let him just try," the darker voice responded. "I wish him all the luck in the world with that."

David kept walking, refusing to answer either voice with his mind or his lips, despite them goading him to do so. During his wanderings, he passed a food bank. One of the homeless men in line had a comb-over that appeared to be hiding several bloody patches where he was missing hair. David gasped in horror and quickly looked away.

"You didn't think that hair on your pants appeared out of nowhere, did you, Davy boy?" Perkele mocked him.

David thought about it. It made sense. He had blacked out the previous night, and at some point, he must have attacked this homeless person. Unless there were two black-haired men in Bridgeport missing parts of their scalp, he must have done something to this man.

"I wonder what else he did to that poor guy," a brand-new voice said inside David's head. David wanted his feet to move, but curiosity got the best of him, and he couldn't help glancing at the homeless man again. The man was too busy angling for food, waiting to get his small ration for the week, to notice David.

"It's a good thing he's not turning around," Perkele said. "You don't want to see what you did to his face!"

"Actually, it would be a good idea for you to start walking away right now," said the darker voice. "You don't want him to notice you, do you? How do you think he's going to react when he sees his attacker right behind him?"

For once, David agreed with the voices in his head. He started briskly walking away. But he couldn't resist one last peek over his shoulder. The homeless man was now turned just enough for David to see a blackened and swollen eye socket and bloody bandages over what David assumed was a broken nose. The man's upper lip also swelled, exposing his teeth and revealing that several were broken.

"Why would anyone want to come close enough to heal you, David? You're too dangerous now."

David suddenly felt an uncontrollable urge to hide. Fear gripped him. He was in shock that he had lost control of himself enough to do what he had done to the homeless man. It was a fear stronger than he had ever felt—something primal. He only made it another block before running behind a dumpster and hiding deep in its shadows. Curled up in a fetal position, David didn't feel even remotely safe. Emotions usually had no sway on David, but now, fear seemed to have a stranglehold on him.

When David finally drummed up enough courage to return to the dorms, he walked past no less than three officers of the peace and two campus security boys on his way there. His nerves were frazzled by the time he got to his dorm room. None of the cops seemed to have paid him any mind, but the entire way from the dumpster to the dorm room, the voices inside David's head howled and screeched at him.

Glad to be safe inside his dorm room, David didn't even care that Richard was there. Though sweating and breathing hard, David attempted to look calm and collected. He silently nodded to Richard, and Richard nodded back. Then, David sat down at his computer.

Pulling up an Internet browser, David wasted no time searching the name Ophelia Carter. Soon, he was watching videos with his headphones plugged in. Richard seemed too preoccupied with beer and video games to notice. As he continued to search, David found thousands of webpages about Ophelia, maps with directions to the Safe Haven, instructions on what to do when you arrive there, and other relevant information.

As he dug deeper, David found a video of Ophelia curing a mentally ill person like himself. The woman was so far gone when she met Ophelia that her eyes were rolled back in her skull. But by the time the video was done, she was looking directly at people around her, speaking clearly, and touching the corners of her smiling lips with delicate finger taps. David knew why she was doing that because he was experiencing the same thing. He hadn't smiled in so long that if he started smiling now, his lips would be sore to the touch.

David stared at a map with a bright green pointer marking the Safe Haven and memorized as many details as he could. Then, he quickly shut it before the voices had a chance to return and spy on him. He had no intent of letting them talk him out of what he was planning to do.

Chapter 25

D AVID WALKED TO the Greyhound station with the financial aid money he'd saved up. He purchased a bus ticket for Springfield, Missouri, which was the closest Greyhound stop to Blue Eye. "Think again, David!" Perkele shouted. But David pretended not to hear him.

David planted himself in a seat toward the back of the bus, at the end of an aisle by the bathroom. Just as he had hoped, no one else sat anywhere near him. He pulled his baseball cap down over his head and tried to relax. But the bumps and bangs and the atrocious smell of the bathroom made falling asleep a distant fantasy.

The bus emptied out at least once a day, and everyone had to wait for a connecting bus. While everyone else tended to stay inside the Greyhound station, David hovered around the grass and trees outside, enjoying the sweet air and the sounds of the city.

On the last bus ride—from Kansas City to Springfield—the voices started up in earnest. "You're really going to get rid of me?" Perkele asked.

"You can't escape what you did!" the darker voice shouted.

"You'll never make it! We'll stop you!" the newest voice chimed in.

Each voice had different qualities that distinguished them. And the evil hatred inside every voice brought David's anxiety to the surface. He tried to stay calm, but the closer he got to Springfield, the more vivid the threats became.

"If you even think about going into Safe Haven, I'll take over, and you'll start hurting people in the audience," Perkele warned. "I'll even make you injure Ophelia."

"Here we are, folks. Springfield, Missouri!" the bus driver said through the overhead sound system. "All passengers, prepare for disembarking and luggage transfer!"

It had been a long trek from Kansas City, and David doubled over when he stood up. The only thing that saved him from completely falling was the headrest that doubled as a handle on the seat in front of him. He pulled himself upright, but he was filled with fear and anxiety that he couldn't control. *He wasn't in control.* The thought haunted him. Maybe normal people could handle being out of control, but David couldn't.

Getting off the bus without any luggage, David immediately started thumbing a ride, and he found Missouri to be much friendlier than Connecticut when it came to hitchhiking. A pickup truck pulled over less than a block from the Greyhound station, and it took him the rest of the way to the Safe Haven. David didn't even mind that he was surrounded by ropes and dirty rakes. Air whistled past his ears as they sped through farmland, and David couldn't hear the voices over the wind, no matter how loud they howled.

Chapter 26

OPHELIA NOTICED A strange young man lurking in the audience, staring at her. At one point, someone bumped into him, but his unblinking stare stayed trained on Ophelia. He didn't even waste a second to look at the person who bumped him.

Ophelia knew the stranger needed healing. She wondered why he had not attempted to approach her to ask for it, but she never pressured anyone to the stage. She found that most people were afraid of her at first, and she figured people would approach the stage when they felt the time was right, only coming up when they truly felt safe.

Eventually, David did walk to the stage. He was completely alone, with no supporters accompanying him. And no friends waved to him from the audience. Ophelia could tell how lonely and afraid he felt. She was familiar with being lonely and afraid, having been ignored by her parents when she was younger, and this commonality with the stranger particularly tugged at her heart.

Once Ophelia was able to look into the young man's eyes, she felt a deep rush of satisfaction and relaxation. She almost never had that feeling when she was about to heal someone. Instead, she usually felt anxiety and a little nausea each time she was preparing to leave her body and enter someone else's. She had never felt love and compassion like this when looking at someone in need of healing before.

"My name is David," the young man said. His hands shivered in spite of the blistering fall weather that the air conditioners were failing to eradicate.

"Don't be scared, David," Ophelia comforted him. "I'm going to heal you."

David leaned back in the healing chair as Ophelia's hands went around his head. But his shaking wouldn't go away. The golden healing light beamed out from Ophelia's hands as usual, but when it reached David's scalp, the light started to dim and turn muddy. Ophelia's eyes widened. She hoped that the audience wasn't seeing the same thing she was.

Breathing deeply, Ophelia forced more power into her hands. The beams of light glowed brighter, and before long, the glowing light penetrated David's brain. Ophelia was now inside him. Once there, Ophelia took note of the crowded environment inside David's head. Many different entities other than David battled for control of his headspace. She could sense their fury.

Ophelia tried to focus on the most annoying voice first. The voice was from a strange creature that kept fleeing to the dark shadows in the corners of David's mind. A deep swamp clung to the sides of his mind, and Ophelia waded through it, searching for the creature. Spotting the dark thing lurking by a clump of ferns, Ophelia sent her healing energy full force.

The healing light tore through the dark creature like a laser beam, whistling with energy. Ophelia kept stabbing golden light into the darkness of the swamp, and when the creature's screaming stopped, she turned her attention to other entities—ones that were still unseen but far from unheard. The voices tormented and taunted Ophelia. They didn't willingly dare to show their faces, but Ophelia trudged through the swamp, hunting down every last one of them until all the evil voices had been silenced.

When all the voices were gone, Ophelia was about to exit David's head when she encountered a small baby floating in the swampy water. She lifted him out of the water and into an imaginary boat. For some reason, Ophelia felt a strong connection to David's inner child, which was now a toddler who was smiling at her. As the threads of David's mind wove in and out of the swamp, glowing like fireflies, Ophelia reminded herself that it was time to leave.

Ophelia slowly pulled herself away, tendril by tendril, until the fibers of David's brain were smooth and clean. She trekked through space and time to return to her own mind. The journey took longer than usual, but when she got back to her body, she could see that David was smiling from ear to ear and putting a finger to his lips. "The voices are gone!" he shouted. "I can't believe it!"

"Yes," Ophelia confirmed. "And you'll never suffer from those voices again. You can go home now." David walked off the stage without another word. It was the end of the day, and everyone would be leaving the Safe Haven soon.

After closing, Ophelia returned to her private quarters and fell asleep, beginning to restore her energy. But when a noise woke her up prematurely, an unexpected visitor stood nearby.

It was David. "How did you get in here?" Ophelia asked. She was surprised not to feel even the slightest bit alarmed.

"I have my ways," David said.

"Well, it doesn't matter. I'm glad you found me. I want you here with me."

"Good, because I want to be here," David answered.

"I've already healed you. Is there something more you need?"

David smiled. "I want to know what your life is like."

Ophelia exhaled slowly. "It's fine, I guess. There's nothing wrong with it, I mean."

David perked his eyebrows up. "Nothing wrong at all?"

Ophelia paused to think. "No, nothing wrong at all. I'm the greatest healer the world has seen since our Lord and Savior, and I haven't suffered any of the ills that he encountered. So, why would I have any problems?"

"Does everyone who comes here have to pay the regular ticket price?" David asked.

"No. Those who cannot afford it are provided for by the Healing Hands Foundation. Their tickets are paid for from our ticket revenue, as handled by my mother."

"And where does the rest of the ticket revenue go?"

"To my parents, of course," Ophelia answered.

"So, you're the one doing all the work healing people, but the money is going to your parents?"

Ophelia laughed, shaking her head. "Yeah. What's wrong with that?"

"You're twenty-one years old, Ophelia. Why is your mother handling *your* money?"

"Don't be absurd, David," Ophelia responded. She was suddenly feeling a little offended by the stranger's probing. "A lot of parents take care of their children's money."

"Yes, but you're not a child anymore, Ophelia." David's eyes seemed dark and serious.

As Ophelia took stock of herself in her mirror, she remembered that her little girl days were long over. A strong, mature body had developed while she was healing people. Her body had new desires now—desires that ran counter to her mission as a healer. "I see what you mean, David. I'm no longer a child," Ophelia conceded. "But I'm far too busy to take care of my own money anyway."

"And whose fault is that?"

"I don't know what you're trying to get at, David. It's my passion to heal people. Without this gift, I'm just another regular person. Why shouldn't I let people take advantage of my healing powers as much as possible?"

"You just summed it all up right there, Ophelia. 'Taking advantage': that's exactly what everyone around you is doing. They're taking advantage of you. Oh, God, Ophelia, you've been so sheltered that you just don't get it, do you?" David ran his hands through his hair. His face was downcast.

"No, they aren't taking advantage. I *want* to help people by healing them. And my parents simply pushed me into the limelight while helping me do so. I never expected this to become a career that makes money, so the fact that it has doesn't bother me."

David shook his head and laughed. "But you missed your entire childhood! Did you ever get to play? Did you ever get to have any fun at all? You've missed out on so much, Ophelia. What about a first kiss? Or prom night? Or even just a first date?"

"I'm way too busy doing healings to worry about things like that. In fact, I have many healings to do tomorrow, and I usually use this time to restore my powers to full strength. So, I'm not sure how much longer I can go on having this conversation."

"Is that reasonable?" David continued to prod, raising both his eyebrows very high and questioning. "Rebuilding your power every night just to give it away again? Think about it, Ophelia! Have you been deprived of free thinking for so long that you can't even tell me what *you* want out of life?"

"I know *exactly* what I want. I want a nice, quiet picnic by the lake after work so that I can just unwind and relax without any pressure."

"Well . . . I can make that happen for you, Ophelia. I've got the perfect place in mind, actually. Why don't I pick you up after you're done tomorrow, and we can just take it easy together?"

Ophelia hesitated and thought. She had just met this person, and yet she did not feel the slightest bit of unease around him. "It's a plan," she confirmed. "But please go for now. I need time to myself, to raise my energy."

"I'll go, then," David agreed, backing away toward the door.

"Yes, please go," Ophelia said again. "There are people who need my power." David kept backing away but not quite fast enough for Ophelia. "You heard me," she snapped. "If I have to tell you again, there's no picnic!" Despite her tone,

Ophelia knew David meant well, and though she didn't want to admit it—to herself or to David—she was actually quite charmed by him.

After David left, Ophelia wanted to sleep more, but she couldn't stop thinking about everything he had said. *Maybe he's right*, she thought. *Maybe I'm overworked and taken advantage of.* As she began to concede these points to herself, she suddenly found new, deep channels of raw energy that she hadn't thought of tapping into before. All of the energy she had tapped into so far was healing energy that brought her peace, but this new energy brought a surging . . . fury.

As the new power grew, Ophelia's entire body started glowing bright gold, and she noticed the overflow of energy in the mirror. She allowed two beams of light to shine around her hands before closing them off again and reserving her power for the day ahead.

Chapter 27

T HE SIGHT OF DAVID wearing sharp clothes gave Ophelia newfound energy after a long day of healing. And his smile as she took his arm drove her exhaustion so far that her legs were tingling with excitement by the time they reached the nearby lake.

David arranged a lavish picnic by the lake, on a part of the beach that was shaded by massive overhanging oak trees. He was happy to be in fine clothes with a good woman by his side. Children playing in the water caused splashes and shrieks, but nobody seemed to notice Ophelia and David's hideaway further up the beach. Ophelia felt content, and even Paivatar's absence for the moment didn't change that.

"This was so thoughtful, David," Ophelia said. "It's just what I needed. Thank you."

"You're so welcome," David answered. "What better place to show you my gratitude for healing me?"

"You're the first person who's ever really listened to me, David. You found a place where it's quiet and private, and we can enjoy the miracle of nature. You gave me exactly what I asked for—exactly what I wanted. Thank you so much."

"It's not a problem. Really, Ophelia, it's not. It's the least I can do for the woman who healed me."

"Well, now that I've started to relax, I know for sure that I've been working too hard. Why else would I have snapped at you yesterday? That's not like me at all. Please accept my apology."

David shook his head. "No need to apologize but thank you. My counselors always told me that my troubles were caused by me acting out ills I'd witnessed in my life. But when you cured me, I realized that the forces I dealt with were way beyond my control. How did you gain the power to heal people?"

Ophelia felt her walls coming back up. Her past had become a closely guarded secret. Her parents had changed the patter years ago to stop mentioning the angel's name so that all the focus was on Ophelia instead. "I don't really want to talk about it, David."

"Why not?" he asked.

"I had a wonderful day today, and tomorrow is probably going to be even better. Can't we just focus on that? My healing powers come from a divine source, and you don't need to know any more about it."

"Why not? Why is it such a big secret?" David continued to prod.

"I don't want to talk about it because I had to die for twelve minutes to get my powers!" Ophelia blurted out. With the truth on the table, her walls were pointless. Ophelia felt them coming down like missile bay doors, sliding away into the recesses of her mind. "It's not this incredible miracle like my parents make it out to be. No, I just drowned for twelve minutes—because of them, actually."

Ophelia felt her long-buried memories making their presence known. She suddenly remembered her body slowly float-ing to the surface of the muddy water. She hadn't thought about it in years. Even though Ophelia was a good distance away from the lake, looking at the water made her shuffle further up the blanket. She felt defenseless without her walls in place.

"It's okay," David said. He reassuringly cupped his hand over Ophelia's. "You don't have to tell me anything more right now. Just . . . whenever you're ready."

Ophelia gave David a forgiving kiss on his cheek. "This warm air is making me so sleepy," she said, yawning and stretching out on the blanket beside David. As the exhaustion of the day overtook her, Ophelia fell asleep.

* * *

David enjoyed the remainder of the picnic as Ophelia slept. He preferred the potato salad, so that disappeared first. As he continued chewing, the voice contacted him to check in. "You pushed her too hard!" Perkele shouted. The shouting was loud enough to cause David to cover his ears. "I warned you about that. You almost scared her off, you amateur!"

"Shut up!" David snapped.

Ophelia stirred on the blanket. "Are you talking to some-one, David?" she asked.

"No," David answered in a whisper. "Go back to sleep." Ophelia immediately dropped back into a deep sleep.

David leaned back against a tree and finished the rest of the potato salad while the voice kept screaming in his head. "What were you thinking, you fool?! Stop talking to me out loud!

Sometimes, I think you *want* people to find out about me. But you wouldn't dream of that, would you?"

David kept his mouth shut. But Perkele continued needling him anyway. "Honestly, boy, you sound like a crazy person when you talk back to me. Do you want people to think you're schizophrenic? Do you really want Ophelia to know that you still have voices in your head? That would be a disaster. Our whole plan would be ruined."

David wanted to talk back but kept resisting the urge. The more Perkele embarrassed him, the more resolved David was not to speak. Nevertheless, Perkele kept hounding him.

"I picked *you* because you know about the long plan. If you let on that I'm still here, she'll just go inside your head again and ferret us all out. We lost some perfectly good demons during the healing session. Yes, they were weak—none of them possessed realms half as fearful as mine. But if this terrible girl can get rid of them, she can get rid of me. Do I have to explain my entire plan to you again?"

David remained silent but kept his mind open, listening. Perkele continued: "Make her fall in love with you so you can pull her away from the ones who care about her. Once you do that, get rid of the energy in her head that's stopping her from being afraid and doing bad things. She has more power than anyone I've ever seen. You have no idea how much evil she's capable of. If we can flip her to our side, she has enough power to help us turn my realm into a living, breathing entity that will destroy the entire world."

David remembered the plan he had agreed to. But he still felt somewhat horrified at the idea of the whole earth being decimated. Perkele's teeth had sunk so deep into his soul, though, that David had no control over himself. All he could do was nod and listen. David's fear had made him a prisoner to Perkele.

"Just keep working at tearing her down. But take it slow, you moron! Go too fast, and you won't get to learn about her weaknesses. Keep your wits about you. She still has a lot of strength." Seeing Ophelia waking up, David stretched like he'd been napping too. "I'll be back!" Perkele shouted. "Don't screw this up!" With that, Perkele's voice disappeared.

"Did I fall asleep?" Ophelia asked. David nodded but kept his smile inside his lips. "I'm sorry," Ophelia said. "I've ruined your picnic."

"No, you haven't. It's all right, Ophelia. You deserve your rest. God knows you need to rest more than anyone else needs it."

Chapter 28

THE DAY AFTER the picnic, Ophelia got back to healing. She began the day as steadfast and determined as
ever, but a new weariness soon crept in. It started with stiffness
in Ophelia's arms between healing sessions. Then, the heavi-
ness turned into an iron lump in her stomach, pulling her down
into her chair. Every time she came back to her body after a
healing, her legs were all pins and needles, as though her
circulation was being hindered.

Ophelia was far more exhausted than usual, and she struggled through the day. To make things worse, for some reason,
Paivatar never showed up to reveal to Ophelia the people most
in need of healing. So, Ophelia had to make the hard decisions
of whom to heal on her own. She was now immensely popular
the world over because of her appearance on *The Kathryn
Cornich Show*. And five different times that day, Ophelia had
to choose one of three different people in need to heal. She was
not sure whether she had chosen the ones most in need, but the
others were out of luck regardless.

At the end of the day, Ophelia pulled the energy back into
her hands and noticed that there was even less left than usual.
And as soon as her head rested on the back of her chair in her
dressing room, she was out like a light. When she woke up,

daylight was streaming through the windows of the Safe Haven. She had still not seen Paivatar. It was the longest Ophelia had gone without communing with Paivatar since she was first given her powers.

Some of Ophelia's power had returned overnight, but it was nowhere near her usual levels. "I knew there would be days like this," Ophelia told herself in the mirror as she was getting ready. "Paivatar will come back. I know it." Ophelia stared at her face in the mirror as though she were looking for some sort of visible confirmation from herself that what she was saying was true. But all she saw was her eyebrows raised in defiance and aggression.

Suddenly, there was a snarling sound and a smash, and Ophelia's mirrored face lay shattered across the floor, with dozens of reflections of her eyes blinking back at her. In the reflections, she could see that circles of red stained her face, and she turned her right hand over to find bleeding knuckles.

Pushing golden light through her body, Ophelia healed her own cuts, though she knew she wasn't supposed to. Anger still plagued her, compounded by the knowledge that she had wasted energy healing her own body. First, she had snapped at David. And now, she had purposely shattered her mirror. It had only taken a few days without Paivatar for Ophelia to see that she wasn't as strong as she thought without the angel's help. *What's happening to me?* Ophelia wondered.

No matter how hard Ophelia tried to solve the riddle, she could not figure out where her anger stemmed from. She decided that her separation from the angel only resulted in frustration, not aggression. It was not the source of her anger.

No, something deeper was at play—something that made her want to lash out and hurt even herself.

Ophelia's uncertainty continued to plague her all day, even after she had healed over forty people—by far the most she had ever healed in one day. The last person for the day said her name was Isobel. She was a little girl who had waited all day with absolute patience for the chance to be healed by Ophelia. The girl had a phobia involving neckties.

Isobel sat in the chair across from Ophelia and immediately reminded Ophelia of her lost childhood. Ophelia shook her head and did her best to push away the raw emotions she was feeling. She slowly entered Isobel's mind and began freeing the dark tendrils of a phobia from hidden niches in the girl's cerebellar neurons. But anger continued to linger in Ophelia's mind, and a small bit of it escaped into the young girl's mind. The anger manifested as a shadow darting across a paradise of flowering trees.

Ophelia was astonished as the small shadowy figure cavorted through the trees, completely ignored by the girl but tracked by Ophelia from meadow to meadow. Where had it come from? Was this thing what had been causing all the havoc in Ophelia's mind?

The shadow didn't look like any sort of known creature to Ophelia. Instead, it looked more like a troubled spirit. And this troubled spirit left blackened, rotting grass in its wake and trees that withered into dust. Ophelia was certain that this thing was meant to distract her from completing the healing. Shooting tendrils of golden light at the shadow, Ophelia saw a puff of smoke rise from the point where she focused the light, and the shadow disappeared.

When the shadow had disappeared, Ophelia suddenly caught a glimpse of a girl being strangled by a necktie. Before Ophelia could decide what to do, the girl had been strangled to death. But a few seconds later, the strangulation vision began again, and Ophelia used her healing energy to tear the tie in half before the girl could die another time. Another tie suffered the same fate, and then another, and another until the ties stopped appearing around the girl's neck. Ophelia wasn't sure what the source of Isobel's necktie phobia was, but she was satisfied that she had dispelled the nightmare it was creating.

Ophelia left Isobel's mind. Isobel sat up in her chair and opened her eyes, with her mother hovering over her. Ophelia looked at them with a peaceful smile. "Thank you for healing my daughter," Isobel's mother said.

"Of course. I'm so glad I could help!" Ophelia responded.

"Let's go, Isobel." Her mother ushered her off the stage.

As Isobel and her mother walked away, Ophelia tried to ignore the tightness in her neck and shoulders. She waved goodbye to the audience as the show ended, but her shoulders cracked and popped with each swing of her arms. Later, as she slept, she was again deprived of dreams. But some of her energy had returned, and she was confident it was the good kind of energy.

Chapter 29

FOR THE NEXT two days, Isobel avoided her usual panic attacks associated with seeing neckties. Then, her doctor made a house call one evening to see how she was doing. "How nice to see you here in person," Isobel's mother, Jenny, greeted him.

"It's my pleasure," the doctor responded. "It's important for me to see her in her usual environment for something like this," he explained. "I need to see how she behaves when in the presence of ties to know for sure that she's been cured."

Jenny led the doctor and Isobel to the master bedroom. "Her father's ties are right over there, in the closet." She motioned to a door at the far end of the room.

As Isobel stared at the closet door, Dr. Marks opened it with infinite care, as if the treasures of the realm slept inside instead of silk ties, nylon ties, and bowties. With the ties now fully displayed, Isobel did not show the slightest sign of panic. The doctor wasted no time in declaring her healed. Jenny hugged Isobel with joy.

On the third night after seeing Ophelia, while Isobel slept, she had a terrible nightmare. It started out peacefully enough, with lots of teenagers getting ready for a dance. But the deeper Isobel went into the dream, the darker it got. For one thing, when she went up to the mirror to put on lipstick, she saw a boy's face staring back at her, and she realized she must be a boy in the dream. Because she was a boy, someone handed her a tie, and the dream-boy tied it around his neck with ease. After smiling at himself, he walked onto a dance floor and started mingling with a crowd of other teenagers.

When the music started, the boy felt his pulse quicken, and his neck swelled. He tried to push the tie away from his throat, but the more he tugged, the tighter it got. Pain shot through his face, and with the burning pain of suffocation came the tingling of nerves all over his face.

At that moment, Isobel opened her eyes, but not a word escaped her lips. In total silence, she lifted out of bed and walked into the living room, grabbing a pair of crafting scissors off the living room table as she went. Creeping into her parents' room without waking them, she retrieved her father's ties and carried them out to the living room.

Isobel twisted a red and white striped tie in her hand, playing with the fabric. Then, with a loud snip of the scissors, she cleaved the tie, and it tumbled to the floor in two pieces. Grabbing a second tie, Isobel did the same thing. The "schwick" sound of the slicing scissors was amplified in the dead silence of the middle of the night. The sound was enough to rouse Jenny, who arrived in time to rescue Hank's commemorative labor union tie from destruction. She whipped the blue and gold tie away from Isobel with a loud snap, and Isobel cut into thin air instead of the tie.

A small ocean of half-ties swam at Isobel's feet. Jenny snatched up the remaining full ties before Isobel could get to them. Then, Isobel did the strangest thing Jenny had ever seen. Isobel reached to where the pile of ties had been, picked up an invisible tie, and started trying to cut the thin air under her clenched hand.

"Give me that!" Jenny shouted. She grabbed the scissors, trying not to slice Isobel in the process. But Isobel wouldn't give them up. Her elbow remained locked and defiant. "You're too young to play with those scissors, young lady. You could hurt yourself." Jenny kept her voice low to keep from disturbing her husband, Hank, who was short-tempered. She hoped she would have time to discard the sliced ties before Hank saw them all over the floor.

In a voice two octaves lower than her usual voice, Isobel growled out, "I'm not going to stop until every last choking necktie is gone!"

Jenny was now terrified. "Let . . . GO!" she shouted, lowering her voice to match her daughter's sinister tone.

"No!" Isobel shouted in an even deeper voice. The growling sound she made as she spoke made her sound more like a feral animal than a human.

Hearing the noise, Hank came running into the room. "What are you doing, young lady?!" he shouted.

Jenny got distracted by Hank's shout and lost her grip on the scissors. With otherworldly force, Isobel's hand snapped back. One blade of the scissors buried itself into the palm of Isobel's other hand. Isobel yanked the scissors out, and Jenny could see Isobel's tiny finger bones poking through the muscles the scissors had torn. Blood spurted onto the carpeted floor. Somehow, Isobel's strange trance continued unabated.

"Isobel, wake up!" Jenny shouted. "Oh, God, Hank, we've got to get her to the hospital!" Isobel's eyes still had a half-lidded effect. Jenny knew plenty of sleepwalkers, and when they would stub their toe or step on a Lego piece, the pain would snap them out of it. But Isobel seemed like she was still sleepwalking as she continued reaching for the invisible pile of ties.

Jenny scooped Isobel up in her arms and carried her to the car. The entire way to the car, Isobel's undamaged hand kept reaching out for more ties to cut. Her other hand dangled below her, with blood dripping off it and onto the grass.

Isobel sat on Jenny's lap while Hank jumped into the driver's seat. Even in the car, Isobel continued reaching for ties. "She cut up almost all my ties!" Hank shouted.

"That's not what's important, Hank!" Jenny shouted back. "Can't you see something's wrong with her? Not just her hand, I mean—something else."

When they reached the hospital, Hank opened the door for Jenny. She had already forgiven him for his earlier frustrations. Jenny wasted no time rushing her daughter through the emergency walk-in doors.

The damage to Isobel's hand was immediately obvious to the nurses as they approached her. "Maggie, go get a patient history form, would you?" one of them said.

A passing doctor decided to lend a hand. He lifted Isobel out of Jenny's arms. "Let's get this girl prepped for surgery!" he shouted. Maggie watched the doctor back through a set of swinging double doors with Isobel cradled in his arms. She could hear him shouting orders as they went. "If we act now, we can still save her hand," he continued. "But she's also having seizures. We'll need a CT scan as well."

Maggie turned to Jenny. "Since your daughter's already getting prepared for surgery, I'm going to need you to answer these questions as fast as you can. Your name?"

"Jenny," she answered.

"Your daughter's name?"

"Isobel!" she sobbed.

"Has anything like this happened before?"

"She's had nightmares. But this looks more like sleepwalking. She used scissors to destroy almost an entire closet full of ties before I could stop her. And then, she put the scissors right through her hand like she couldn't even feel it!"

"So, she's never had a sleepwalking episode?"

"No, never!"

"Has she had seizures before?"

"Oh, God, never! I didn't even think about that!" The bang of a door opening behind Jenny made her jump in her chair.

"You can see Isobel now," the nurse who walked through the door said. "Come on back."

"How is she?" Jenny asked, getting up.

"She's been stabilized. And she's been sedated to slow her arm movements. But we don't have all the test results back."

As they walked through the noisy back corridors of the hospital, Jenny's mind spun. Visions of the terrifying scene involving Isobel plagued Jenny. And now, her poor daughter was deep inside a massive hospital, waiting for her to arrive. Jenny had no idea what to expect when she got to Isobel's room.

When Jenny reached the room, she was relieved to see that Isobel's eyes were fully closed. Isobel's breathing was deep and slow, but her tie-grabbing arm seemed to be lifting up and down independent of her breathing. It only moved a couple of inches off the bed at a time before coming back to rest. Isobel's other arm now had a bandaged hand and was resting on her belly. It rose and fell with each breath, providing a counter-rhythm to the restless, tie-grabbing arm.

"What's wrong with her, doctors?" Jenny pleaded for answers. "Why won't she wake up?"

"We're not entirely sure. In full disclosure, we haven't seen anything like this before. At least . . . not in people. It's something that's more common in animals. Have you ever seen a dog chase something in its sleep?"

"Yes, Rufus always does that."

"Well, it's like that with your daughter. She's having a dream, but she's acting it out. Even under general anesthesia, she kept fighting back. We had to sedate her for our safety and hers. She was fighting us with her good hand, even under local. Even with the sedatives, you can still see that her hand is moving a little."

"Yes, I see," Jenny confirmed.

"As long as her hand is moving, the dream is still happening. She's still deep in sleep. She can't hear any of us. All we can do is wait for her to wake up. I think we need to prepare for the possibility that it could be days before that happens."

"Well, you might have time to wait," Jenny said, "but I don't. That's my daughter lying in that bed!" Noticing that Hank had joined them, Jenny turned to him and asked, "What are you going to do about this, Hank?"

"I'm going to tell Ophelia Carter exactly what I think of her healing practices!" he angrily shouted.

"Hank, no. Stop thinking that way!" Jenny scolded him. "Ophelia is a world-famous healer. There's no way she's responsible for this."

"She's a con artist is what she is," Hank shot back. "And I'm going to confront that con artist about what she did to our daughter!"

"Hank, don't make a fool of yourself!" Jenny continued to plead. "Just stay here and take care of Isobel!" As she saw Hank turn and stomp away, she erupted in sobs. "He's just going to make it worse," she cried to the doctor.

"I agree with you," Dr. Dodge said reassuringly. "I've seen Ophelia's healing with my own eyes. She's no con artist, and there's no way she could hurt anyone . . . not intentionally, at least. There's something else at play here. Something—or someone—else is hurting your daughter."

"Why didn't you say something sooner?!" Jenny sobbed out. "Hank already left!"

"I was trying, but he never gave me a chance!" Dr. Dodge shot back.

Jenny sank into one of the visitors' chairs next to Isobel's bed and never took her eyes off her daughter until she was so physically and emotionally exhausted that she dozed off herself.

Chapter 30

OPHELIA STOOD ON stage, preparing herself for another day of hard work at the Safe Haven. A boy in need of healing had just sat down on the chair in front of her. The heat from the skylights beat down on Ophelia. And even with the air conditioner going full throttle, the August heat from outside added to the warming up of the entire building. She hadn't even started, and she was already feeling exhausted.

A familiar man walked into the audience sprawled out in front of Ophelia. She knew she had seen him before, but she couldn't remember where. He caught her eye because he kept walking toward the stage instead of taking a seat like the other audience members. Ethan and Marilyn spotted him too, and they stepped in front of him before he could reach Ophelia.

Ethan and Marilyn had the man by the arms, but it was clear he had no intention of calming down. "Can't you see she's a fraud?!" he shouted at the boy in front of Ophelia. "Can't you people see it?!" he shouted, addressing the audience this time.

Without his tie, Ophelia hadn't recognized the man as Hank. But when he started talking, his voice brought his name back to her in a heartbeat. "What's going on, Hank?" Ophelia asked him.

"How can you deny it? You're a fraud! Ophelia Carter is a fraud!"

Ophelia tried to remain calm. "I really don't know what you're talking about, Hank," she replied. "I am *not* a fraud!"

"Really? If you're such a great healer, then tell me why my daughter is in the hospital right now! She was here to see you just days ago."

"She's *where*?!" Ophelia cried out in shock.

"She's in the hospital right now. And she won't wake up."

"All she saw me for was a phobia about ties," Ophelia countered. "How could that possibly land her in the hospital?"

"She had a nightmare while sleepwalking. She cut up almost every single one of my ties and then stabbed herself through the hand with a pair of scissors. She was supposed to get better after seeing you, not worse! You're a fraud, Ophelia Carter! You didn't cure my daughter at all!"

"But *my* child got better after seeing her!" a mother cried out from the crowd. "He couldn't walk before he came here. Now, look at him!" She gestured to the boy next to her, who stood up with ease. The boy sauntered around the room, using his recently healed legs to explore every space that was not full of chairs.

"And my daughter was healed just last week!" a father cried out. "She's just fine now, but we keep coming back to see the miracles. I've never seen my daughter so happy."

Rather than calm Hank down, the denials only enraged him more. "If you healed these other people, then how come you can't fix my daughter?!" he shouted at Ophelia.

"Now, Hank, let's just go in back and talk this out like reasonable people," Marilyn suggested in her most soothing tone.

Hank readied himself to protest. But Marilyn was done up like a Southern belle from head to toe, and her eyes had years of training to perfect a pout and a flawless stare that brought even the most confident trickster to a faltering confession. Even the outraged father was undone by the persuasive face. He shook his arms free of his captors and stomped to the back room with Ethan and Marilyn following. Ophelia followed as well, after apologizing to the boy in front of her.

When they were all in the room, Hank slammed the door behind them in one last show of angry force. But behind closed doors, he became a somewhat calmer man, filled with pain and doubt. "My little Isobel had a phobia about my ties," he reminded the Carters.

"Yes, I remember," Ophelia said. "It was a particularly memorable healing for me. It happened about three or four days ago."

"Yes. And I've never seen her so happy and confident as she was in the days after seeing you. But last night, she started cutting my ties in half in the middle of the night. And when Jenny, her mother, tried to stop her, she fought back and ended up stabbing the scissors into her hand."

Ophelia tried to keep her tears inside. But when she heard the story, the tears burst forth of their own volition, and she could not hold them back. "I'm so sorry," she said through her tears. "I've always been terrified that a day would come when there was someone I couldn't heal."

"What in the world is wrong with you?" Hank asked. "You're supposed to be a healer! Isobel's doctors were able to get the scissors out of her hand. And they've got here sedated in some sort of sleep. But she still hasn't woken up, and they don't know when or if she will."

Ophelia stared at the floor, deep in shock. The tears continued welling up in her eyes.

"Hank, our daughter has spent her entire life healing people," Marilyn interjected. "Her healings have been well documented. She's never *not* healed someone. So, I'm sorry, but what you're saying seems impossible. Think about it, Hank."

"Well, if Isobel's nightmare wasn't left over from before Ophelia attempted to heal her, then where did it come from?"

"It could have been from any interaction or experience Isobel had in the days after seeing Ophelia," Marilyn proposed. "It could have even been from someone or something she interacted with in our audience after she stepped off the stage. Legend has it that nightmares can jump from victim to victim."

Hank hung his head, shook it from side to side, and put his fingers on the bridge of his nose, pinching it. He stayed that way for several seconds. He stayed that way so long that Ophelia thought he was going to pass out. But he eventually pulled himself together and said, "All right, I don't know what's going on here. But it seems like Isobel is possessed or something!"

"Please let me try to heal her again, Hank!" Ophelia insisted. "Even Lazarus had to wait days before Jesus could heal him a second time. Please, let me try."

"And why would I do that after the damage you've already caused? Isobel was worse after she saw you than before. How do I know you won't make her even worse this time?"

The stress of the situation was turning Ophelia's shoulder

pain into sharp cramps, and she cried out, "I'd be happy to go to the hospital and try again! Please!"

"No!" Hank roared. "I don't want you anywhere near my daughter!" With that, Hank ran out of the Safe Haven.

Ethan went to the stage and said into the microphone, "I'm sorry, but we're unable to do any healings today." A deep hum ran through the crowd. "If you all come back tomorrow, admission will be free, and the healer will be able to take care of your needs then." The audience members slowly got to their feet and made their way toward the exits.

Ophelia, hearing her father's words as she stood in the back room, dropped her head and folded her hands in prayer. "I always appreciate your support, Mom," she said, "but I really need some time to myself right now. Can you please give me time to think? The audience has given me that respect. Can you, Mom?"

Marilyn could not hold her tongue. "You watch yourself, young woman! God might have given you those healing powers, but *I* am the one who brought you into this world and worked hard to help make your dreams come true! What makes you think I don't respect you?"

Ethan had returned to the room just in time to hear his wife's words. He put his hand on Marilyn's shoulder with kindness, but she jerked like a demon had grabbed her. "Let her spend some time with Paivatar," Ethan said. "I'm sure she'll be all right in the morning."

Marilyn took in the longest breath Ophelia had ever seen. When she finished taking it in, she reluctantly said, "All right, I'm leaving. But I'm never going to abandon you, Ophelia, my daughter. Do you hear me?"

"Come on, Marilyn, let's go," Ethan urged her.

Marilyn stopped talking and rose to her feet, prepared to stalk out to the lobby. "Sleep tight," she said before following Ethan toward the door. "We'll lock up," she added as she walked out.

"Goodbye!" Ophelia called out through her sobs. The last thing she heard from the other side of the door was Marilyn whispering something like "under a lot of stress." It was one comment too many, and Ophelia felt a tailspin coming on. She felt out of control. She sat down and tried to stop the feeling of helplessness from tearing her apart.

Chapter 31

I SOBEL WAS STILL in her hospital bed with her eyes shut. Her nightmare had still not ended. Her arm kept moving up and down, searching for more ties to cut up. As the rest of her body rested peacefully, the same nightmare played over and over again in her mind. She would pull a tie from the pile, but it would turn into a snake and bite her. She would drop it and then reach for another tie. Without the scissors, she was defenseless against the snakes.

Pulling another tie from the pile, Isobel realized it was the last one, and the snake slithered away without biting her. Her father's closet that had housed the ties shattered into hundreds of pieces in front of her eyes, and a whirlwind lifted her free of her nightmare. She heard the beeping of a hospital monitor and knew she was awake.

A shadow formed on the end of one of Isobel's bare feet, below the hospital ankle tag. It was the nightmare, and it was preparing to find another host now that its latest victim had broken free from its grasp. Without her terror, the nightmare's grip on her was spoiled. Without the fear, the nightmare was powerless. The nightmare expanded itself in the air around Isobel's foot, and it finally detached from her, oozing down the metal leg of the hospital bed and disappearing across the floor.

Isobel's mother didn't even notice the odd shadow sliding away because she was too busy pounding away at the nurses' call button at the sight of Isobel's eyes being open. After that, the shadow was out of sight. "Isobel's awake!" Jenny shouted into her phone. "Get back here, Hank! . . . What? I told you not to go to the Safe Haven! You're going to apologize to that poor girl . . . Yes, of course you're going to apologize to her!"

As the shadowy nightmare slunk away, it contemplated entering Jenny. But the nightmare only wanted people who would hurt their own bodies, and Jenny radiated the need to hurt other people, like the man she was yelling at on the phone. Jenny would not be a good candidate. Her rage was directed at other people.

The nightmare needed someone with deep self-confidence issues so that it could control them through their own fear. As the nightmare slunk into the hallway, it spied a likely target. There was a nurse who walked with pain in every step she took. Here nametag read *Ms. Choate.* A crushing attraction pulled the nightmare toward her with incredible force.

The demon stole across the distance between itself and the nurse, and it surged into her ankle, desperate to haunt a new victim. The nurse's body accepted the shadow without noticing anything. Hannah already suffered from too much pain to care about a small prick in her ankle. Every one of her toes felt like it was broken at the end of her shifts, and her hips felt ready to separate.

Hannah Choate only wanted to lie down in bed and fall asleep after her shifts. She had no time for children in her life, and the one child she did have was long gone—college life had separated them. So, Hannah enjoyed the solitude of her apartment without ever needing anything to fill the silence. Anyone who wanted to date her would be dating a woman who sleeps all the time when she wasn't at work. After sixteen hours of work in the hospital, Hannah spent the other eight hours of her day unconscious.

After falling asleep on that particular evening, Hannah had a nightmare about spiders. She already had a deep fear of spiders, and watching them crawl all over the place, in no particular direction, was one of the things that creeped her out the most. Even in her sleep, Hannah felt disappointment that the rest she so desperately needed was being plagued with her deepest fear. As her dread and the volume of spiders both increased, she searched for a way to wake herself up.

In the nightmare, more and more eight-legged monsters covered the floor of Hannah's apartment. She tried to brush them out of the way, but when she did, she just discovered more spiders scurrying beneath. Hannah tried to reason with herself. "It's only a dream," she said out loud as she slept.

The spiders began to crawl on Hannah's arms. The sight of the little creatures and the feeling of their tiny legs on her arms made her panic, and shrieks of horror escaped her. "It's just a dream," she said again. But when she opened her mouth to say it, the spiders got inside, and stings of venom made her tongue burn.

Hannah had never expected anything this brutal to penetrate her dreams. Her usual nightmares stopped when she was endangered. They never went as far as having her die. When the spiders started stinging her tongue, she thought she would be all right, in that crazy dream logic everyone has. But no matter how hard she tried to convince her mind to stop, she swore she could feel real swelling in her tongue.

The swelling in Hannah's tongue pushed against her teeth, separating her jaws. More spiders poured in as her tongue distended from her mouth. She saw the massive, pink, throbbing muscle pouring out of her mouth and tried to scream, but the air wouldn't go past her swollen tongue, and the intended scream instead came out as a weak moan.

When Hannah couldn't get air out, she tried to get air in instead, but that didn't work either. The nightmare stripped reason away from her. Her last thought in the nightmare was about what she could do to get air into her lungs.

Chapter 32

PUSHING HER BODY out of bed in the morning, Hannah knew she couldn't go to work. She had never experienced a nightmare like that before. Even now, her throat was dry, and every breath was fire in her lungs. A horrible taste lingered on her tongue, and even though her mind insisted that it was just congealed dust from the air as she slept, her gut instinct told her it was the venom. She headed for the bathroom to rinse the awful taste away.

As Hannah walked to the bathroom, a little green spider scurried to safety under her coffee table. She screamed and dropped to all fours, staring under the table and shining her phone's flashlight, looking everywhere. But there was nothing hiding under the table at all. Nothing. Hannah squinted in confusion, stood up, and made her way to the kitchen for coffee.

While Hannah was in the kitchen making coffee, she saw another spider scurry across her balcony. She ran outside to squash it, but by the time she reached the balcony, the spider was already gone. She checked everywhere, even leaning over the top of the balcony's railing to check behind it. But the spider had completely vanished. *Spiders don't just disappear*, she had to remind herself.

A third spider scooted out from under Hannah's morning paper when she pulled it from her mailbox in the apartment building's lobby. She shrieked and quickly dropped the paper. But search as she might with her trusty light, the floor remained clear of spiders. "Where are they going?" she asked out loud. *I must be losing my mind*, she thought.

Hannah eventually called the nurses' station. "I'm sorry, but I can't come to work today," she said, faking sniffles and pressing her soft palate to force a nasal tone. "I've got a cold, and I know better than to make everyone else sick." She hung up her phone before her boss could object.

Driving directly to Ophelia's Safe Haven was Hannah's next move. The other nurses could not shut up about Ophelia and her ability to heal people. Though she had never been to the Safe Haven, Hannah already knew where to find it without even having to pull up directions.

Hannah waited all day to see Ophelia. Every time she saw another spider while waiting, she would jump in fear. She had no control over it. A spider would make its presence known and then vanish without a trace. With people sitting all around her, Hannah knew she couldn't indulge her terror by using her phone's light to look for the spiders, or else she might look crazy.

Hannah didn't know which was worse: the appearance of the spiders or the disappearance. Both seemed unbearable, and the feeling that she was losing her mind grew stronger by the minute. Ophelia looked tired by the time she got to Hannah. But she could tell Hannah was desperate and that her nerves were frazzled from the hallucinations. "You have to help me!"

Hannah shouted. "I keep seeing spiders everywhere! I hate those things!"

"I understand. I can help you," Ophelia assured her.

"Really?" Hannah asked, quivering and flinching as another spider ran across the stage of the Safe Haven. Shaking her head in disbelief, she tried to fight off the horrible dread she felt every time an imaginary spider ran past her vision.

Ophelia's hands glowed golden, and soon, Hannah was wrapped in a delicate bliss. Minutes later, the fuzz-covered terrors had completely vanished into thin air, and Ophelia was beaming at Hannah. On her drive home, Hannah saw nothing out of the ordinary, nor when she entered her apartment. It was a huge relief after the day's terrors.

Settling down on the couch in the growing darkness, Hannah found herself in another dream. This time, she was at a petting zoo, and she thought everything would be fine. There were no nightmare elements at all, just bunny rabbits covered in fuzz, llamas that needed trimming, and the same ponies that seemed to be at every petting zoo she had ever visited in real life.

Then, the man running the petting zoo started talking about a tarantula he was holding out to Hannah. There were children surrounding her, but the man was talking directly to her as though she were the only one there. She suddenly recalled that when she was young, this very incident had come to pass, and on her birthday of all days. "Touch the spider. She won't bite you," the petting zoo manager had urged. But the longer she sat in the grass with the tarantula in front of her, the more uncomfortable she had felt.

Hannah didn't want to touch the dream spider at all. It was so big that the zookeeper had to use both of his meaty hands to carry the monstrosity. Two huge stalks, covered in tiny eyes, wiggled in Hannah's direction. She squirmed, got up, and ran away. But as she ran through the grass, it wasn't really grass anymore. Instead, it was covered with huge, crawling spiders, crawling every which way. The mass of spiders was so big that it pushed across Hannah's feet, and spiders started crawling up her legs.

Hannah screamed and tried to move, but the crushing weight of dozens of tarantulas crawling over her feet pinned her in place. Immobilized, she watched as the spiders reached her belly and kept going, up to her face. Her vision was blocked by furry underbellies as tarantulas covered her eyes and stayed there.

Hannah fell backward and hit her head, resulting in excruciating pain. The horrible pain followed her into her waking life, and she reacted to the pain by grabbing her head with both hands and crawling out of bed. She stumbled to the bathroom to get pills for her headache. As she opened her medicine cabinet, she half-expected to find spiders inside. But she was relieved to see nothing but medicine bottles.

A stack of disposable cups sat inside a container by Hannah's bathroom sink. When she lifted a cup from the stack to fill it with water, something shifted underneath the cup holder at the bottom of the stack, and she screamed and dropped the cup into the sink. Lifting the cup holder, Hannah discovered a tarantula hiding beneath it. The spider looked at her with intelligence and jumped for her hand. As she pulled her hand back, she dropped the entire cup holder onto the floor. Leaning over to retrieve the cups, she discovered even more tarantulas were crawling up her legs.

Grabbing a metal pick she used for dental care, Hannah started stabbing the hairy beasts as they crawled up her legs. Many of the swings were misses, succeeding only in jabbing the flesh of her legs with burning pokes. Screams escaped Hannah, but no one could hear her, so no one could respond. She was alone, which was exactly what she had wanted up until this very point in her life.

"Get them off me!" Hannah screamed. "Get them off me!" As the tarantulas moved ever higher, undaunted, Hannah kept stabbing at them. "Get them off me!" she screamed again. "Can't anyone hear me?!"

When one tarantula ran across Hannah's mouth, her biting reflex kicked in, but she missed the spider entirely. She felt its furry feet cross her face, and her phobia amplified every tiny footstep. She screamed and stabbed at her forehead, feeling the pain when the pick impacted bone, but she didn't care. She pounded at her face again and again, desperate to remove the tarantula from her head. "Get off! I said get off!"

Pounding and pounding, Hannah finally succeeded in injuring the tarantula, resulting in tiny hisses and a small bumping from its fuzzy stomach on her forehead. She continued stabbing at her forehead, and the more she stabbed, the faster her own blood ran down her face until she couldn't see anything but a deep red fog. Though the fog prevented Hannah from seeing the spiders, it didn't prevent her from feeling them. And the spiders continued to swarm all over her.

"Get them off me!" Hannah screamed again. Walking blindly through her apartment, Hannah swung her arms to shake off the spiders, but she could not escape them. She felt one crunch underneath her bare foot, but the crunch mixed with a wetness from the spider's insides that made her entire foot crinkle in revulsion as she ran forward, trying to escape the madness all over her body.

Hannah had no idea where she was when she suddenly felt something hard bump into her thigh. She couldn't see anything but a curtain of red, but her ears registered a strong change in orientation with a massive rush of vertigo, and she realized she was falling. She chose to spend her final seconds of life reflecting on the wonderful fact that not a single tarantula crawled across her body during those last moments. They had all been driven away by the force of the air on her body. Hannah's head hit the ground on the sidewalk below her balcony, followed by her body.

Chapter 33

FEELING SAFE IN her back room at the Safe Haven, Ophelia grabbed her phone and dialed her boyfriend, David. He picked up on the first ring. It was something he always did when she called, and she loved that about him. "Ophelia? What's wrong?" he asked. "You're usually asleep by now."

"I can't sleep tonight, David. Something terrible happened!"

"I'm coming right over," David said.

"That would be wonderful. I'll unlock the front door for you."

David left the apartment he was now renting in Branson and arrived at the Safe Haven a short time later. He entered and found Ophelia in her room. She was in her huge recliner, still trying to get her heartbeat back to normal after her encounter with Hank. As David paced back and forth, she said, "David, there's something I have to tell you."

"I'm listening, Ophelia."

"Someone I thought I had healed by eradicating their nightmares wound up in a hospital after seeing me. They had another terrible nightmare, and it ended with them hurting themself in real life. And now, her parents seem to think it's my fault. Her father told everyone in the Safe Haven audience that it was my fault, and I'm scared that they will believe him and start to lose faith in me. Everyone's going to think I'm a failure."

David stopped pacing, went over to Ophelia, and hugged her tightly. She felt secure and understood inside his arms. The voice in David's head whispered with glee, "Now, we have her."

"Oh, Ophelia, I'm so sorry that people are treating you this way. You deserve better," David reassured her. "You're *not* a failure!"

"I failed Isobel, though," she shouted back, pushing David away. "That's the little girl who's in the hospital."

"Ophelia, you need to calm down. Everybody makes mistakes."

"Not me!" Ophelia screamed.

David knew he was in for a long conversation. "Ophelia, now is not the time to lose your self-esteem. Take some deep breaths. We're still standing here, aren't we? The roof isn't caving in, is it? Calm down and try to think rationally." Ophelia stayed quiet, with tears falling from her eyes. "You can't always be butterflies and rainbows," David continued. "Sometimes, people do horrible things to you. Just shine on and let them think whatever they want."

Ophelia wanted to believe David; she really did. He was her boyfriend, after all, and he had taken better care of her than her parents. But she couldn't escape the crushing guilt in her mind. Unable to keep silent any longer, Ophelia started to argue with David again. "But David, what they believe matters to me. If they think I'm a fraud, then they won't show up at the Safe Haven anymore. I won't be able to do what I love anymore!"

"Maybe this is a *good* thing, Ophelia. I mean, what happened to the person you used to be before all this started? Where did the real you go when you took on the persona of a holy woman?"

Usually, David's criticisms motivated Ophelia, but this one tore her down. "That's not fair of you to ask, David! You're not in my shoes. You don't see what I see or feel what I feel."

"Then tell me about it," David urged, sitting down with his hands locked together. "Let me know what's really troubling you."

"When I was in Isobel's dream, I saw something bad running around in there—a creature or demon. I thought I got rid of it, but what if I didn't? What if I can't do my job anymore? My whole purpose is to end people's suffering, not make it worse! How do you think it would make me feel if I couldn't use my gift anymore? Nowadays, I just feel numb, and I don't know how to tell anyone."

"It sounds like you're saying you feel useless—like people don't need you anymore. But *I* still need you, Ophelia. And your parents need you, too. So, you need to keep fighting. You *must* keep fighting. Look how many demons you've defeated over the years before this one! What do you remember about this dream-demon thing anyway?"

"It was short and shadowy, kind of like a leprechaun or something. It was much shorter than the other demons I've witnessed. And it had the strangest laugh I've ever heard."

"Have you ever heard that voice before?"

"Yes! Once before. I've been too afraid to ever tell anyone, but when I was a little girl, that exact same voice told me to go into the water just before I drowned. I didn't know who or what it was, but it had the same kind of laugh that this little shadow thing had. I hadn't made the connection until now. But yes! It was that same creature. What if it's been following me all these years? What if I *gave* that little girl a nightmare instead of removing one?"

"Ophelia, Ophelia. Calm yourself down. I don't think that's what happened. I think it's just that when you let people down, it makes you feel bad. And you've never let anyone down before this. Heck, I've let a lot of people down in my life, but I can't let it get to me. You know why? Because it's too much for one person to handle. But what you still fail to see is how people have been letting *you* down your whole life."

"What are you saying, David?"

"It's like I told you before, Ophelia. Here you are doing all this good, but you are surrounded by people who are using you or doing bad. Take Father Henry, for instance. From what you've told me and what I've seen in my short time living here, he treats homeless people like objects and turns them away from his church. I've never seen a preacher be so rude to poor people before! He's committing a sin, Ophelia! He's not doing the right thing."

"So, what am I supposed to do about it? I didn't choose these people; they chose me?"

"I'm saying that if you have a skill—a power—you should use it to your advantage in whatever way you can. I'm saying that in addition to healing people, you should hurt those who hurt others."

"David, that's evil! I'm not going to hurt someone just because they hurt others. That's not the way God would want it."

"Well, an eye for an eye is right there in the Bible, after all. And I haven't heard you talking to the angel in weeks. She's abandoned you, too, Ophelia."

"I might be naïve, and I might not know everything," Ophelia responded, "but I do know that Paivatar is real and that she'll find a way to speak to me when she can."

"So, you admit it. Even the angel has now turned its back on you. I'm the only one left you can trust, Ophelia. I've been in your corner ever since I got here. In addition to your healing power, you have the power to punish people who walk all over you and over others. Now that people are turning on you anyway, why not use that power as well?"

Ophelia was starting to feel her back against the wall. "No, David. The angel will come back someday. And when she does, she's not going to be happy if she knows that I abused my gift!"

"You're wasting your time, Ophelia. Your angel isn't coming back. When God turns his back on you, he's done for good. I don't know why you keep holding out hope. I keep trying to tell you that you already have all the power you need."

Ophelia took several heavy breaths before responding. "I'm not going to give up just because people are starting to turn their backs on me. I'm going to keep healing the faithful, and everything will turn out for the best." Ophelia knew she was slipping back into earlier ideals, but she couldn't help herself.

"Ophelia, you said it yourself: you're passing nightmares on to people now. So, you might as well send the nightmares to people who deserve it. Leave all the suffering fools behind and go after the evil pricks who deserve to be punished. You can start with Preacher Henry."

"I'll think about it, David," Ophelia conceded. "I'll really think about it."

"You'll do more than think about it," David responded. "You'll do it, because you love me, and you know I'm telling you the truth. And I'll know you did it when I see in the papers that something has happened to Father Henry. I promise I won't be the only one congratulating you when that happens."

"I told you, I'll take it to heart, David. Yes, I'm sure all the homeless people he's harmed would be happy to see him suffer."

"That's my girl," David said. "I knew I could count on you!"

David left the Safe Haven, and Ophelia returned to her resting chair. After a lot of thought, she decided David was right. It was time to give Preacher Henry a nightmare that he would never forget. Ophelia slipped into the land of dreams, searching for Henry's signature. She knew he would be deep inside a good dream around that time of night.

Chapter 34

OPHELIA LOCATED A good dream Father Henry was having, and she slipped inside it. His dream was easy to find because, even in his dreams, his mind projected visions of himself being in better shape than he actually was. His mental praises for himself echoed far beyond his dream and out into the strange dream-ether Ophelia was floating through, allowing her to detect it. She heard his signature at once and advanced her mind to his location, shimmering through the thin membrane of his dream bubble.

In Father Henry's dream, he was stepping out the door of his favorite coffee shop with a hot cup of tea in his hands. It was his favorite moment of every day. Ophelia felt no pity for the vain preacher as he stepped across the parking lot to his Bronco with confident strides. She began to flit around the dream, implanting ideas into the heads of all the people around Father Henry who he had shamed or ignored. Her suggestions were crystalline and brilliant, and the people had no problem listening to her suggestions.

Ophelia sent a special suggestion to a woman who was turning on her Ford truck and idling the engine while she talked on the phone. It was just a simple nudge, telling the woman to start driving, but it was enough to send the truck rolling to its inevitable fate. Back in Ophelia's chair in the real world, a smile formed on her face.

Father Henry kept crossing the parking lot, content and satisfied. As he got close to his Bronco, he turned, but he had no time to react to the cherry-red Ford barreling toward him. The woman behind the wheel still had her cell phone pressed against her head with one hand while she drove with her other hand. Henry looked like he was about to scream, but the truck sucked the wind out of his lungs when it collided with him.

Ribs broke with popping sounds while the distracted driver dragged Father Henry sideways, with his shoes bouncing against the pavement like bad wheels on a shopping cart. The truck veered to the left, continuing on its wayward journey. It careened across the parking lot before eventually crashing into a tree. Henry fell to the concrete, bouncing off his shattered ribs and rolling onto his back.

Father Henry panted, with his lungs rattling from built-up fluid. Hundreds of people walked up as he suffered. It was all the people he had ever hurt in life. "Help me," he wheezed out. "It's hard to breathe." Back in her chair, Ophelia squealed with glee at seeing Henry scared for his life.

The people around Father Henry stood watching him with their arms crossed. Not a single one of them pulled out a phone or waved down an emergency vehicle. "Why aren't you doing anything?" Father Henry asked. "Can't you see I'm dying? Get some help!"

"Well, where were you when we begged *you* for help?" the entire crowd of people asked at once in a zombie-like monotone. "What did you do when we cried at *your* door?"

"But that's different!" Father Henry shouted. "None of you were dying. *I'm* dying here! Won't you lend a hand? Why won't you do anything to save me?"

"Anything helps, sir!" one of the homeless men shouted.

"Won't you lend a dime, sir?!" a homeless girl added.

"We need a ride, please. It's raining, and our car broke down!" another person said.

"I'm so hungry, and you have all that food in your church. Can't I just come inside?!" begged another.

"None of that is the same," Father Henry argued. "You can't come to church dressed the way you're dressed. It would be an insult to God. I'm dying here."

"*You* are the one who's an insult to God, Father Henry!" one of the homeless men shouted. Maggots crawled through the man's beard, and what teeth remained in his mouth had deep infections. "You're a slave to sloth!" the man continued. "Everything you do worships his evil name! You turn away homeless people. You don't help the people you pass in the street. You don't even let us have the food your congregation doesn't shovel down their throats. Your Lord—the one you preach about every weekend—said to suffer the little children to come to him! You ought to be ashamed of yourself. Standing by and not doing the right thing is a deadly sin, Father Henry. You of all people ought to know that!"

Henry's breathing accelerated, and blood sprayed from his teeth with each ragged exhale. "Don't you have anything to say for yourself?" the homeless man asked him.

"It hurts to talk. Please, just save my life," Henry whispered.

The crowd stood motionless. There was no sound, other

than Father Henry's ragged gasps for air. "So long, Father Henry," the homeless man said.

Chapter 35

OPHELIA WAS NERVOUS THAT Father Henry would figure out the source of his nightmare. She dressed earlier than usual and left the Safe Haven to visit a park she knew Father Henry usually drove past. After sitting on a park bench for some time feeling depressed, with her arms crossed, she finally saw Father Henry pull up in his Bronco. He opened the passenger-side door and begged Ophelia to get in. "You need to see this!" he shouted, with tears dripping from his face.

Ophelia got up and jumped into Father Henry's car at once. They drove the rest of the way to the coffee shop where Father Henry liked to get tea, and when they arrived, there were more homeless people than ever standing by the porch. Father Henry parked, jumped out, and started walking the queue of homeless, handing out money. "I've got plenty!" Father Henry called out as he laughed a little nervously. "And don't worry, ladies and gentlemen; you are all welcome in the house of the Lord! I hope to see you at church this very day."

Ophelia was beyond surprised at the generosity Father Henry was showing. She thought that if her dream tampering had any effect on him at all, it wouldn't show for several weeks. But here he was, handing out money to the homeless and . . . ordering them food! "I need sixty blueberry muffins and sixty triple-shot espressos," he told the shop's manager. "That should be one for every man and woman on the property. If you don't have that many muffins on hand, I'll pay extra for you to make more."

"You got it," the manager agreed. "God bless you, Father Henry. You seem like a . . . changed man."

"Indeed, I am," Father Henry confirmed. "I hope to see you at church today. And God bless you as well." Henry turned to Ophelia. "Come on! Let's get to the church!"

Ophelia finished her coffee on the way to Baxter. She had been exhausted from the happenings the night before. But by the time they reached the church, she'd regained her fire. A short time later, homeless people started showing up in droves, having been brought over in the coffee shop manager's pickup truck. Each group of homeless men and women was deposited in front of the church with enthusiastic honking from the truck's horn. Father Henry greeted each group that arrived by saying again, "You are all welcome in the house of God!"

Father Henry gave each group of homeless that arrived a different task to help out with. Once inside, several of the homeless men set to breaking eggs, while one man—clearly a cook before he was homeless—slapped bacon on the fryer and slapped the sausages down too. Henry had planned on cooking alone, as he usually did, but he welcomed the extra help.

Soon after Father Henry and the homeless people finished breakfast, the church's council members began showing up. The discovery of homeless people inside the church caused quite a stir among the council members as it seemed to go against Father Henry's long-standing dress code. "Hello, everyone," Father Henry greeted the council members after they had all arrived. "I know there are more people here than usual, but that's something you might need to get used to!"

Some nervous laughter ran through the room before Father Henry continued. "You might have noticed that some of the people attending breakfast this morning are a little down on their luck. It wouldn't be right if we did nothing to help them, so they are all getting free food today. They even helped prepare your brunch today. So, would you all please give them a warm welcome?"

"But, Father Henry, you know that their kind never wash their hands!" Sally Decker, who was a council member, called out. She didn't seem to care that the homeless men and women could hear her.

"You let those filthy bums touch our food?!" a council member named John yelled. He turned to look at the rest of the council. "Don't worry, folks. We can just order pizza for today."

The homeless people started moving toward the food again. "Shoo! Shoo!" Sally shouted while using her purse to push some homeless men out of the way of the food. "Don't go near our food! You don't deserve to touch it!"

"They probably already contaminated it anyway," John posited. "So, just let them have it! Who cares if *they* get sick?" John turned to Father Henry. "You started all this, Father Henry! We never asked for any of this! You're fired!"

Without a word, the preacher stomped off toward his basement office. Without the preacher, the council sat stunned and rudderless. "Well, we definitely have to get a new preacher," Sally pointed out.

"And I'd like to see a new custodian for the kitchen duties," John added.

"I agree," Sally said. "When this is all settled, we need to have an emergency meeting. Don't anyone plan on going anywhere. Except for you homeless people. You need to leave now."

Ophelia sat in stunned silence as the council members paraded around on the church's stage, wandering from side to side and discussing their all-important church business while the entire church fell to shambles around them. This wasn't what she had planned at all. The homeless people were supposed to go home happy. The church was supposed to accept Father Henry's newfound grace with open arms. In her darkest imagination, Ophelia had never thought the council members would deprive a man of the cloth of his own church.

Ophelia knew that some demon had a hand in all this. Without Paivatar, Ophelia's brilliant light had diminished to a corrupted, faded shade of its former glory. And without her full powers, Ophelia knew she would be helpless against whatever demon had snuck into her life.

Preacher Henry emerged with a box of his belongings. Before leaving, he turned to the council members and said, "I hope you all have horrible nightmares tonight!" No one other than Ophelia seemed to pay him any mind. To Ophelia, the sting of what he said was personal, and she felt her dealings had been exposed in spite of no one turning her way.

"Get them away from the food!" Sally shouted as the homeless men and women started tucking away brownies and cookies.

"This is absurd!" another council member yelled. "You're all hypocrites! These men and women deserve food just as much as the rest of us." With that, a huge quarrel erupted among the council members and between council members and homeless men and women. The entire room was in chaos.

Ophelia was shocked again. How could all this happen from one nightmare? Now, word would get out that there was no preacher and that the church council was in disarray, and no one would want to worship there.

All Ophelia had wanted to do was embarrass the preacher. She didn't want to destroy the entire church. People worshipped God there. She had destroyed a place of God—the God who had been so good to her in giving her healing powers. As Ophelia retreated from the church, she felt her own worst nightmare was coming true: a world where her powers were no longer useful.

Chapter 36

A S OPHELIA WAS LEAVING the church, she couldn't help but notice a headline on the local paper lying on the steps: *Local Nurse Stabbed by Unknown Assailant.* She was horrified to see that the photo accompanying the story was of Hannah Choate, who Ophelia immediately recognized. Picking up the paper, she read further:

> *The Branson Police Department responded to an emergency call last night. Officers arrived at the scene at 8:52 p.m. to find the victim, Hannah Choate, a nurse at Mercy Urgent Care, had fallen from the balcony of her apartment. Numerous puncture wounds from a sharp object had been inflicted on her face. The Branson Police Department was unable to comment or provide further detail on the investigation at this time.*

By the time Ophelia finished reading the article, her hands were shaking. She ripped the article out of the paper and shoved it into her pocket. After looking around to see if anyone had noticed, Ophelia started walking away as fast as she could. As she walked to her parents' house, she whispered with dismay, "I caused this." Tears welled up in her eyes. "This is all my fault," she whispered.

By the time she reached her parents' house, Ophelia's hands were still shaking, but she had steadied them enough to knock on the front door. Marilyn answered and ushered Ophelia to the dining room table, where her mother and father had just finished lunch. Ophelia immediately threw the article onto the table in front of them. "You raised a murderer!" she shouted.

Ethan snatched up the article and began to read. Ophelia tried to wait patiently, but her fists were balled up, and she was gasping for breath. Her impatience made her heart pound until she had to sit down across from her parents, with her hands outstretched on the table to steady them. Ethan tried to reason with her. "It doesn't say she was murdered, Ophelia."

"That woman is dead because of me, though!" Ophelia sobbed.

"Ophelia, what are you talking about? You heal people, not kill them." Ethan looked confused.

Marilyn spoke up. "Ophelia, please try to calm down."

"Hannah's blood is on my hands! This is not what I wanted. I never wanted my gift to kill anyone."

"How do you know this was your fault?" Ethan asked. "How could you possibly know what really happened? It says here that the nurse fell from a balcony and had puncture wounds from a sharp object. It sounds like she was murdered, yes. But are you saying *you* stabbed her? Are you saying *you* pushed her off the balcony?"

"No, Dad, you don't understand. That nurse came to the Safe Haven. She was one of the people in need of healing. I healed her—or at least, I *thought* I did. She complained of having horrible nightmares about spiders, but she seemed fine when she left the Safe Haven. I thought for sure I had healed her. But my gift has been acting so strange lately, and I've been *feeling* strange. I think my gift has been hurting people lately."

Ethan shook his head. "Nonsense, Ophelia. I've seen all the evidence I need. She already had the nightmares when you healed her. You didn't give her the nightmares, and if you're suggesting that the nightmares didn't go away, well, that's not your fault either. It's not your fault, Ophelia."

"But how do you know I didn't make her nightmares *worse*?" Ophelia sobbed. "You can't do what I do, see what I see, or feel what I feel!" Her hands started to shake again as she cried.

Marilyn put her hand on Ophelia's shoulder, and Ophelia let it rest there. "Your gift still has so many people to help, Ophelia," her mother assured her. "You can't give up now, just because of some small obstacles. God gave you your gift, and you know God would not have done that to this nurse. Do you think God would hurt someone intentionally? Of course he wouldn't do that. Now, come on; you have to get back out there and heal people. Lots of people still need you!"

Ophelia pulled away from her mother's touch and raised her hands defensively. "I can't, Mom! What if I get someone else hurt or killed?"

Marilyn's tone suddenly became sterner. "You listen to me, Ophelia Carter. If you don't get back out there, we won't be able to pay the bills, and there goes the nice house and . . . the Safe Haven! We already explained that you can't possibly be causing nightmares. It's all in your head."

"Your mother's right," Ethan agreed. "Just get some sleep,

and you'll feel better tomorrow."

"No, I will not!" Ophelia protested. "I won't try healing another soul until I know for sure that my gift isn't causing harm! *You* don't have my gift! So, how could you possibly know what it is or isn't doing?"

"But what about all the people at the Safe Haven, waiting to be healed by you while you wallow in doubt and self-pity?" Ethan asked. His flaming red ears gave away the emotions he was feeling. "You're not acting like the daughter I raised right now," he continued. "I guess you'll have to explain everything to them yourself, won't you?"

"Ophelia, please be reasonable," Marilyn begged.

"No, Mom! I'm not facing them anymore!"

Ethan was now shouting. "Listen to us, you ungrateful little girl! These doubts are all in your head! Just go back to the Safe Haven so we can get back on track!"

"*You* can go to the Safe Haven if you want," Ophelia shouted back. "But I'm never showing up there again!" Ophelia stormed out of the house, slamming the door behind her.

Once outside, Ophelia took a deep breath. She was proud of herself for standing up to her parents. But she realized that her parents would be mad at her now, and she decided the best place to hide was at David's apartment. She got into her car, which she always kept parked at her parents' house since she rarely left the Safe Haven other than with David. Turning the engine over, she could smell oil burning a bit, but the engine seemed to have held strong after all the years that had passed— strong enough to get her to David's house, she figured. She backed out of the driveway and sped down the road, with a loud squeal from the tires.

Inside, Marilyn said, "She's your daughter, Ethan. You have to go find her and talk some sense into her."

"I've known Ophelia her entire life. There's no talking reason to her right now. If you don't have the heart to talk to her yourself, then I'll have to go to the Safe Haven and explain to everyone there that Ophelia needs a couple of days off. I'm sure she just needs to cool down a little before she's ready to talk to us."

"Fine, you do that, you lazy bastard!" Marilyn shouted. "Go waste your time down at your precious Safe Haven. You heard her; she's never going back there! Not unless you talk some sense into her, that is. You make sure you get Ophelia back there, you hear me?!"

Ethan slammed the door behind him, too. Marilyn sat in solitude contemplating their situation and . . . their bills.

Chapter 37

ETHAN DROVE TO THE Safe Haven, where several dozen faithful stood outside with confusion and impatience all over their faces. He stepped out of the car and cleared his throat. The silence he faced was uncomfortable, and he wanted to get this over with as soon as possible. "I'm sorry, but you'll all have to go home," he announced. "The great Ophelia Carter will not be appearing here today. She's not well and needs some time to recover."

Ethan had sincere hopes that his words would be enough to satisfy the lingering people. But instead, shocked cries of anguish erupted from the faithful. "I came two thousand miles to see Ophelia!" one woman shouted.

"Well, I'm visiting from Canada!" another person shouted.

"I came here all the way from *Brazil*!" a man shouted. "What are we supposed to do now?!"

"Please calm down, everyone!" Ethan pleaded. "Branson is wonderful. Just stay around town until Ophelia is ready to see you. I'm sure she will be back very soon!"

"Well, let's get back to the hotels, then," the man from Canada suggested to his wife. Everyone started getting back in their cars and taking off.

Ethan got back in his car and waited for all the other cars to clear the parking lot. Then, he scribbled a note with a red felt pen and secured it by the entrance to the Safe Haven for anyone else to see. *Closed for Vacation—Please Come Back Soon!* it said.

With his mission complete, Ethan drove away in the opposite direction from town, hoping nobody would chase after him. When he got home, Marilyn was exactly where she was when he left, waiting for him. "Did you do it?" she asked.

Ethan swallowed hard. "Yes. I closed the Safe Haven, Marilyn. It's done."

"I failed her, didn't I?"

"No, of course not. What are you talking about, woman?"

"I pushed her too hard, Ethan!"

"Don't blame yourself for this mess. This was *my* fault, Marilyn! I should have protected her better. The second David showed up, all of this Safe Haven business went south! Did you notice that? I should have never let those two get close to each other."

Marilyn tried to soothe Ethan, but he was still angry with himself. "If that's true, Ethan, then it's *both* our faults. A mother should always watch out for her daughter. Always! We neglected her again, Ethan—just like we did when she was little." Marilyn sat slumped in defeat. "We *both* failed her!" she said, with a finger pointed at Ethan.

Ethan could not argue against Marilyn's logic or her pointed, shaking finger. "Well, maybe we neglected her in the *past*. But this time, we did everything we could to keep her from walking out that door!"

"Did we, Ethan?" Marilyn challenged. "*Did* we?" She got

up and paced back and forth.

"She's an adult, Marilyn! What else can we do? We can't *make* her come home."

Marilyn lost her temper. Flying into a complete rage, she grabbed Ethan's shirt collar and used it to pull his neck, head, and face down toward hers. Ethan had no choice but to look into his wife's face as she stared him down, with fear for her daughter turning into a possessive rage. "Listen to yourself, Ethan!" she yelled. "You've turned into a coward! You're scum! You're a complete fraud and a chicken! You can't protect your daughter, you can't protect the business, and you're going to stand there and tell me you can't even protect your wife?!"

"Marilyn, it's not like that!" Ethan cried out in defense. "I'm doing everything I can! You know I can't put Ophelia in a cage! She's a free woman!"

Marilyn released her good hand from Ethan's collar and used it to smack him across the face. He stared at her in silence, praying she would come to her senses before she knocked him out. "Bring my daughter back to me!" Marilyn screamed. "If you even want to call yourself a man, you're going out there with me to find my daughter and bring her back home where she belongs!"

Marilyn ran outside, with Ethan trailing by a few steps. "Be a man," he muttered to himself as he struggled to keep up with his wife. Their car raced down the driveway with both of them inside, and they didn't share a word as the tires hissed across the pavement.

Chapter 38

DAVID LET OPHELIA into his apartment on her third knock. "David, I've hurt someone else!" she shouted, falling into his arms. "They died this time! I can't do the Safe Haven anymore!"

"What?! Who died?"

"A nurse who I healed at the Safe Haven died last night. It's horrible! I can't control these nightmares anymore!"

"Calm down, Ophelia! Tell me what happened."

"Okay," Ophelia said, breathing deeply. "This nurse was having nightmares about spiders, so she came to see me at the Safe Haven to get rid of them. After I thought I'd healed her, she fell off her balcony at home, and the investigators found horrible puncture wounds all over her face and body. I know she was trying to fight off imaginary spiders when she fell because that's what I saw happening in her nightmares. My dad said her nightmares weren't my fault, but what if I made them worse? What if I'm not able to do my job of healing correctly anymore? That would make me a fraud, just like Isobel's father said."

"No, Ophelia. This isn't your fault at all."

"Yes, it is, David. If I weren't famous, Hannah wouldn't have known about me, she wouldn't have sought me out, and she would still be alive."

"But you didn't choose to become famous, Ophelia. It was your mother who shoved you into the spotlight. It was your father who shoved you into the spotlight. It was . . ."

"Pete Reed!" Ophelia shouted. "My goodness, I'd forgotten all about him. It was Pete Reed! *He's* the one who put me on TV!"

"Who's Pete Reed?"

"I never wanted to be famous! When you're famous, you get hurt sometimes. It's the Devil's work. Personal gain is evil—that's what the angel Paivatar told me. But my parents wouldn't listen to me about that. They forced me into this fame and fortune, and now, I'm being punished for it. Pete Reed is the head of Reed Global. He's the advertiser who made me world-famous." Ophelia paused for breath.

"So, none of this is your parents' fault; it's Pete Reed's fault. And I don't think you're being punished, Ophelia. Didn't you feel good after you gave that preacher his lesson? He fell from grace, and now, he's paying for it. There must have been something bad about the nurse, too. There must be something she did to deserve what happened to her. And now, Pete deserves to be taught a lesson, too."

"If you're nobody, it doesn't matter if your special powers don't work. But if you're famous, the whole world knows about it. This is a disaster. There won't be one single person at the Safe Haven tomorrow without me there."

David patted Ophelia on the shoulder. He turned her around, and they began to kiss. "Do you want me to stop?" David asked.

"No," Ophelia said, shaking her head. Her love for David overwhelmed her. "No, don't stop. Please, don't stop." David picked Ophelia up and carried her over to his bed, touching her everywhere. "Don't stop," she repeated.

David entered Ophelia with complete confidence, and all of the ills in her mind drained away. It was like being dragged away from a sinking ship. When it was all done, Ophelia hung in a beautiful suspension, like a skydiver not wanting to pull the parachute. Flat on her back, she looked up at David and knew that she would do anything he asked.

"David, something's bugging me," Ophelia said. "I want to give Pete the worst nightmare of his life. But I don't know what that would be for him. How can I find out what his deepest fear is?"

"Have you heard of this thing called the Internet?" David teased. "Everyone seems to be on social media these days. It's a good place to start." Sure enough, after a few minutes of looking, David had located Pete Reed's Twitter page. Half of his posts were about doomsday prepping and survival gear. "He's preparing for the end of the world in any way he can, Ophelia. There's his fear, right there. You now know what scares him more than anything else."

A grin spread over Ophelia's face. "Thank you, my love," she said.

"Are you feeling sleepy?" David asked.

"Doesn't matter if I am or not. I have to enter the dream world to give him a nightmare, don't I?"

Ophelia closed her eyes and wandered into the dream world. Every dream swam through the same world, protected from other dreams by cobwebs floating near them. But through the webs, Ophelia could see inside people's dreams as clear as day. Having worked closely with Pete Reed, his energy was easy for Ophelia to sense in the dream world, and it seemed like only minutes before his face appeared.

Between the strange webs, a bubble of a dream appeared. But Ophelia knew at once that something was wrong. Instead of the usual blue aura surrounding a dream, the material surrounding this nightmare was crackling and dark, obscuring Pete's face inside the dream.

A tugging sensation was the last thing Ophelia expected to feel in the dream world, where everything was some strange otherworld soup and even her own body was just an astral projection, without form or mass. What could possibly be pulling her toward Pete's nightmare? Suddenly doubtful about her plan, Ophelia tried to rein in the new nightmare she had been planning to instill within Pete. But the more she tried to rein it in, the more she was tugged inward until the combination of Ophelia's nightmare and Pete's nightmare brought sizzling energy to the surface of the bubble.

Inside the dream, Pete was drinking coffee and getting ready for the day. As he looked at his refrigerator, Ophelia noticed a handwritten note stuck to the front of it. The note said: *Nike interview, 9:30*. As she looked at the paper, Ophelia noticed water pouring out of the refrigerator. She was suddenly underwater.

The sensation of drowning made Ophelia think of the day she gained her powers. She had never relived the experience in such detail before. She felt rough hands pushing her deeper into the water, and she began to panic as her memory became twisted.

Through the water, Ophelia heard a voice tormenting her. "Now, you get to see what it would have been like if you had stayed dead that day I called you into the water," the sinister voice said. "You never should have come back to life! You should have stayed dead. Now, you've gone too far. You've tapped into powers that are beyond your control, and you've set things into motion that even your Lord and Savior can never undo. Say goodbye, Ophelia."

Tiny dapples of sunlight from high above Ophelia teased her as her soul ripped away from her body, and the moment it left, her pain of drowning was gone. Suddenly, she could see again. Pete was still getting ready to leave, but all Ophelia could do was look. No longer aware of her real-world body, Ophelia knew that something had gone horribly wrong.

Chapter 39

B Y SEVEN IN the morning, Pete had finished shaving his stubble off with a straight razor. He ran the razor under a stream of hot water to rinse away the stubble, and then he rinsed its head in the water pooling in the sink's basin, stirring it. Suddenly, the water started turning black and running down the drain. Black goop burped up from the drain and filled the sink with burping liquid that foamed against the sides of the sink, staining the white porcelain.

Is he still asleep, having a nightmare? Ophelia wondered. *Or is he really awake and hallucinating?* Without a body, she felt powerless to escape Pete's mind. All she could do was watch.

Pete was horrified. He dropped the razor into the garbage and tried to run the tap to clear the disgusting liquid from the sink. Clear water poured out of the tap again, rinsing the awful mess away. Pete grabbed a new razor and went back to shaving.

While getting dressed, Pete felt a tremendous rumbling underneath his feet, and he didn't know where it was coming from. It sounded like the earth was trying to break apart beneath his apartment. Pete's dress shirt had a lot of buttons, and while he wrestled with the tiny buttons, his eyes wandered to the wall. The shaking continued beneath his feet, and the wall was starting to crack apart. "Good God!" he said. "I've got to get that fixed."

The crack in Pete's wall grew wider with each moment. Soon, the plywood behind the plaster started poking through. Then, the plywood split in half, and Pete covered his head with his arms, trying to shield himself. The longer he waited for the ceiling to collapse on his head, the less he shook. Lifting his eyes, he discovered the wall was completely intact again.

Nightmares can't happen when you're awake, Ophelia reasoned. *He must still be asleep.*

Pete finished getting the tiny buttons in order. He grabbed his briefcase on the way out the door and headed to his Ford Explorer. Remembering that the corner coffee shop served triple espressos, he decided he would head there before the interview. One of those, or maybe three, would do the job.

Driving down the road, Pete noticed a man in his passenger seat. *Where did he come from?* Ophelia wondered. The passenger had brass soldier's insignias on his uniform, but napalm had ruined the fabric, and the insignia was branded into the charred flesh of his chest.

"Hey, Pete. Remember me?" the mysterious passenger asked. "I'm Simon, your father's friend from the war. You and I have a lot to talk about, buddy."

Pete's hands shook on the steering wheel as he drove. Before long, he wiped the sweat from his palms against the upholstery in the Explorer. "You're not real," he said as he drove. "You can't be real."

"Believe what you want," Simon said. "But I'm right here."

"I thought you died a long time ago. You've been burnt to a crisp, and it smells like you just got extinguished! How are you even talking?"

"Your life is more complicated than you think, Pete. The dead still walk the earth. Most people just can't see us."

"My father worshipped you. He told everyone how you sacrificed your life for him, rescuing him from the enemy."

"He told you that, did he?" Simon asked.

"Yes, he told me. It's because of you that I decided against joining the Marines. My father told me I could never be half the Marine you were!" The ends of Simon's jawbone poked through his charred skin. Pete shivered against his will and kept driving.

"I'm glad you didn't join the Marines, Pete. If you had, then maybe you wouldn't be alive and talking to me."

"You don't get it. I never got the chance to be a hero!" Pete shouted. "Don't you see that you're just a reminder of everything that I couldn't be? You gave your own life so that my father could escape the battlefield alive. Without your sacrifice, I wouldn't be here. I could never live up to that. To his dying day, my father couldn't stop reminding me how I owe my life to Simon. The last word on his lips was your name—not mine, not the Lord's, and not my mother's. What he said was, 'Why couldn't you be more like Simon?'"

"Oh, that's what he told you, huh?"

"Yes, that's what he told everyone. He was so proud of you!"

"That's total bullshit!" Simon shouted, causing his jawbone to come loose. "You didn't know your father at all. He's no war hero! He was a coward—a dirty stinking coward!"

"Don't you call my father a coward!" Pete shouted.

"Don't believe me? How do you think I got burned up? Your father abandoned every soldier in his unit! He ran away like a coward! Sure, two of our gunners were already dead. But four brave men still stood ready to fight. And what did your father do? He ran back to the commander to call in an airstrike! The next thing you know, it's not some enemy cutting my throat, it's a ball of fire coming out of the sky—from my own side. It's called 'friendly fire.' But ya know what? There's nothing friendly about napalm. No, sir!"

"I'm sorry about what happened to you, and—" Pete stopped talking when he saw that Simon had suddenly vanished. Pete realized he was in the coffee shop's parking lot. He shut off his car's engine and deeply inhaled and exhaled for a long time.

Suddenly, the bitter aroma of roasting coffee permeated Pete's nightmare. Ophelia was surprised to find that she could smell it. The coffee shop was crowded, and Pete stood in line impatiently. As he waited, he kept looking out the window, and Ophelia tried to see through his eyes as the nightmare cut in and out like a fuzzy radio station. Each time Pete looked out the window, the scenery had changed.

This is getting way weird, Ophelia thought. *Even for a nightmare.*

Suddenly, a three-cylinder gas tanker in the parking lot was struck by lightning. The lightning struck the middle tank, and a chain of explosions ripped the tanks to shreds, blowing debris stories into the sky. The shock wave rolled across the parking lot and shattered the coffee shop's windows, tearing them away. But none of the customers inside cared or even looked up from what they were doing.

Pete lifted his hands to absorb the impact of the rolling explosion, and his elbow bumped the man in line ahead of him. "Hey, do you mind?" the man asked.

Pete looked at the man, ready to apologize. The man's acne-scarred face quivered with rage, and two big tumors stuck out of his forehead, one on each side. Huge veins bulged across the tumors, and the skin of the man's forehead stretched tight across the tumors, pulling his eyelids in strange directions.

Instead of apologizing, Pete rubbed his eyes with his palms and said, "I think I really need my coffee."

"Well, wait your turn!" the man in front of him shouted. He turned back around.

Pete took a deep breath. Looking back out the window, he saw that the scenery was back to normal. Soon, it was just Pete and the strange man in front of him left waiting in line. As the espresso machines shrieked, Pete looked out the window again. The trees across the street burst into flames as a river of lava rolled through them. The sky started to turn red, and Pete was horrified when the lava began rolling against the coffee shop, bringing cars from the parking lot with it and smashing them into the brick walls of the shop.

"There's a lava flow coming!" Pete shouted.

"What are you talking about?" the man in front of him in line responded. "Here, you can have my turn."

"What are you having?" the barista behind the counter asked.

"A triple espresso," Pete said.

"Four ninety-five, please."

Pete dropped a twenty-dollar bill on the table. "Keep the change," he said as he wiped his forehead with a napkin from the counter. Pete looked out the window again and was glad to see that things were normal. He hoped they would stay that way.

"Here's your espresso, sir." A scalded hand pushed a cup of espresso across the counter and toward Pete. Muscle showed through where the skin had been burned away.

Pete looked across the counter in shock. Half of the serving girl's body had been burned. The parts that were burned looked like they had been scalded by hot liquid. Her skin hung in tatters from her arms, and from time to time, a large shred of skin would fall to the floor.

"Don't go to sleep," the barista said.

Pete was so startled that he dropped the coffee cup holding his espresso. When the cup collided with the floor, its weak paper sides collapsed, and the lid sprang free. Steaming espresso sprayed everywhere. "What did you say?" Pete asked.

"I said have a nice day, sir," the woman answered. Her body had not yet returned to normal. Pete closed his eyes, then opened them again, but the hallucination persisted. He knew enough to know that he was seeing things, but he still wanted the vision to go away. "Here's a fresh cup for ya," the barista said, pushing another cup of espresso toward Pete.

As Pete picked up the coffee cup, he heard waves of derisive laughter from the people seated behind him. He was sure the laughter was directed at him. He clenched his fists.

Of course! He's a promoter. He can't stand being humiliated, Ophelia figured.

"Are you okay, sir?" the woman behind the counter asked. She looked normal now, without a single blemish on her skin.

"I'm fine," Pete answered, but his voice was quivering. "Have a nice day."

When Pete turned around to leave, every single patron was staring at him. They were no longer laughing, just staring. Pete was terrified as he took slow steps to the coffee shop doors. Bumping the doors open with his behind, he continued backing up, watching the customers until the doors swung shut. Then, he turned around slowly, holding the cup of coffee like it was the Holy Grail.

When Pete got back inside his car, the passenger seat was still empty. "Goodbye, Simon," he muttered, shaking his head and slurping some coffee. "Go back to Hell."

Ophelia had determined that Pete was not asleep. The nightmare he was experiencing was occurring as real-life hallucinations, making it all the harder for Ophelia to escape it. Escaping Pete's nightmare was no longer a wish for Ophelia but a need. She wanted to reverse her actions in trying to penetrate his dreams, but she knew it was too late to turn back.

Ophelia had always thought that dying was the worst thing that could happen to a human being. But being trapped within another human's nightmare, without any way to get back to your body, was worse than dying. Now that Ophelia's body was long gone, all she could hope was that Pete's nightmare wouldn't get worse.

Chapter 40

WHEN DAVID WOKE UP, he noticed that Ophelia was still asleep beside him in bed. Her chest rose and fell, but only once in a great while. He was curious to know what she had done to Pete, and he wondered if he should nudge her. "Don't even think of touching her!" Perkele screamed. "She's not going to wake up. I made sure of it."

David's mind whirled. "What are the cops going to say when they see her in a coma?! They're going to blame it on me!"

Ophelia's car keys tumbled off the side table. "Just take her keys and drive away, David. Hardly anyone here knows you. Nobody will notice!"

David snatched up the car keys and headed for the parking lot. He was in such a hurry that he left the door to his apartment wide open. He sped away, but as he approached the main bridge out of town, traffic slowed to a crawl, and he saw signs that read *Bridge Construction* along the side of the road. The bridge was a superstructure with room for twelve lanes of cars, but every lane had slowed to a crawl.

"They just *had* to be working on the bridge now, didn't they?!" David shouted in frustration.

Cars stood along the side of the road, with steam pouring

out from under the hoods. Their engines were overheating in the hot sun. With their cars abandoned, the occupants had escaped from the heat in local diners and pool halls.

David kept chugging along with the traffic. When he was the fourth car from freedom, a small plume of steam rose between the suspension wires like a smoke signal, and traffic ground to a complete halt. An overheating car had blocked the bridge traffic, and a tow truck was slowly making its way out onto the bridge to get the car out of the way.

As David stayed parked by the bridge, the thermostat for the car's radiator kept creeping upward. He couldn't turn around as he was boxed in by the cars behind him. He started to panic as the heat level kept going up. The engine was starting to make strange gurgling sounds, and there was a hissing sound coming from somewhere as well. "Come on!" David shouted, banging his fists on the steering wheel.

David didn't want to ruin the engine of Ophelia's car, but he also didn't want to lose the air conditioning. He let the engine keep running even as the loud clicking sounds told him that the piston rods were starting to fail. Once he started moving across the bridge, the engine would cool off. It just wasn't designed for running idle for that long in the endless heat of a Missouri summer.

"Come on!" David screamed again, honking his horn this time. But traffic remained at a complete standstill. David felt his anger reaching terrible peaks, and the air conditioner started to fail, spraying lukewarm air into the car. It was a last-ditch effort from the car to save itself.

David leaned on the horn again, and it made a decent

amount of noise. But the horn was electronic, and with the engine giving up, the honk was broken into little quacks that irritated David even more. Steam emerged from under the hood of the car. The engine gave up entirely, grinding down to silence despite David's foot hammering the accelerator.

Chapter 41

PETE FELT MUCH MORE awake after finishing his espresso, but it had no effect on his strange hallucinations. Just before a new hallucination would appear, there was a strange warping effect, like a mirage, announcing the presence of a new nightmare. Pete couldn't understand how his nightmares were spreading into reality. But he was certain he was the only one seeing them, and he thought it was other people who were crazy for *not* seeing them.

The sparkling paint job on Pete's Explorer—the one he had paid good money for—peeled and flaked away before his eyes. Even the rust underneath the paint blew away in the wind. But as he drove, each time he turned his attention back to the traffic around him, the paint would return to normal.

He shouldn't be driving in this condition, Ophelia reasoned. *It's not safe. He's going to hurt himself or someone else.* Even trapped between worlds, Ophelia never lost her identity. As her challenges kept mounting, she kept fighting back, resisting every effort to lose her mind.

Every car on the roadway seemed to be moving at a snail's pace, with brake lights radiating in a sea of red that would drive a bull out of its mind. "Construction projects. I hate road construction projects," Pete said out loud.

First, he's talking to dead people, and now, he's talking to no one at all. What a lunatic! Ophelia was shocked at her promoter's present state and everything that was happening to him. Sure, she had wanted to hurt him, but everything that was happening to him—each new nightmare that was causing him terror—was also making Ophelia afraid. She repeated Franklin D. Roosevelt's famous line in her head: *"The only thing we have to fear is fear itself."* The quote became a source of motivation for her not to let up and forever be banished to Pete's nightmarish world.

Pete followed the highway around magnificent stands of trees, only to find that Branson's main bridge, the one he was headed to, was completely blocked by an overheated car. Ophelia focused on the sequence of events, trying to sort out what was real and what was in Pete's mind while trying to ignore the terror in her own mind. As she did so, Pete noticed a detour around the bridge, snaking off on a nearby road. "A detour?" he said out loud. "I'm never going to make it to the meeting on time!"

Pete could see inside other cars as traffic turned into stop-and-go. But he wished he couldn't see inside because all the drivers had burns and peeling skin across their faces, as though the sun had burnt them to a crisp in their cars. Police cars passed from time to time, pulling past Pete in the median. But even though their sirens were blaring, he couldn't hear them.

He can't even hear the sirens, Ophelia noted. *The nightmare is completely breaking his grip on reality!*

Pete was prepared to take the detour past the bridge, but some sort of monster was now sitting inside his car, laughing and pounding on the dashboard. The creature had long horns and hands big enough to crush the doors of the car. "I'll destroy you, you monster!" Pete screamed. "I know you're the one behind all of this!"

Pete plunged his foot down on the accelerator and attempted to weave around the cars in front of him. But he ended up slamming into a stalled car—*Ophelia's* stalled car, with David still inside. Destruction followed at once, with Pete's head smashing into the windshield but his seatbelt stopping him from fully going through it. Pete rocked back and forth in his seat, unconscious.

Ophelia's car hurtled forward past the flagger. The car was on a direct course toward the edge of the bridge, careening across the pavement and slamming into other vehicles as it went, as though it were a cue ball. David stayed rooted in the driver's seat, gripping the steering wheel with both hands. The car was moving so fast and David was so panicked that his foot kept missing or slipping off the brake pedal as he tried to jam it down.

The bridge's guardrail offered no resistance at all, shattering against the car's radiator. The car flew over the edge of the bridge and sailed in what seemed like slow motion to the river below, with David still holding onto the steering wheel the entire way down. He didn't expect the impact to come as fast as it did, and when the car hit the water, his seatbelt slammed against his ribcage so hard that it knocked the wind out of him. The seatbelt vibrated as it pinned David inside the car.

White bubbles of escaping air slid across the windshield as the front of the car sank into the water. When the back end entered a few seconds later, David felt intense vertigo as the car suddenly leveled out. David tried to open the door, but the force of the water held the door in place. Dark, muddy water covered the car, and all David could see outside was a thin glow from the sun. Within the vehicle, the gloom was complete enough to obscure the door handle that he was frantically pulling.

David realized that he had no control over the situation. He was filled with dread. As water leaked in, it began to cover the top of David's shoes. As the water crept higher, it was so cold that he could no longer think straight at all. Pure panic kicked in as David realized he was drowning. He pushed the buckle of the seatbelt with all his might, and the seatbelt released. He knew that the space between the windshield and the dashboard would be the last air pocket in the car, and he put his face there immediately.

David's calves cramped in the cold water, and then his knees shriveled as the icy water covered them. He pounded on the windshield as water advanced past his waist, and his heart began to pump faster from the shock of the icy water. A shadow sunk out of the dim glow from the sun above David, and whoever the shadow came from began pounding on the windshield. Despite them pounding with all their force, the windshield did not crack.

David watched, helpless, as the shadow floated back into the murky water above him. He knew that by the time the person came back down for him, it would be too late. He floated in the water as it covered his torso, and he angled his face to the windshield, trying to get as much air as he could.

The remaining pocket of air flooded with water as David arched his neck in a precarious way, trying to grab one last breath. Then, the pocket disappeared altogether, along with David's hope.

Now, two shadows floated down through the murky water, but David found them obscured by some sort of purple dots in front of his eyes. Unable to cry out for help with his mouth, David screamed in his mind to Perkele. But Perkele didn't answer him. David felt completely abandoned. And the abandonment took away his will to keep fighting.

As David lost control of his diaphragm, air bubbled out of his lungs in a long underwater scream. His final choice was to suck all the water in at once or to instead inhale the water a little at a time, giving him a few seconds longer to live. Either way, David knew this was the end—he was going to die.

As David sucked water in greedily, the pain in his heart from his body's struggle for survival was excruciating. He counted the seconds until his end. Just before a loud POP separated David from the world for good, Perkele's sinister voice returned. "Goodbye, David. You've served your purpose."

Chapter 42

ETHAN AND MARILYN DROVE slowly through the neighborhoods of Branson, searching along the sidewalks, desperate for any trace of Ophelia. They figured she was with David, but as their relationship with their daughter deteriorated, she never disclosed where he lived. It was part of the strange hold that David seemed to have over their daughter ever since he showed up at the Safe Haven.

"We should be looking in the main part of town," Ethan suggested.

"We've already been all over town!" Marilyn cried. "Where else should we look, Ethan: the gravel pits or the U-Haul lots? Just keep looking anywhere for any sign of our daughter." As they continued rolling down the road, Marilyn noticed something glinting in the parking lot of a rundown apartment complex. Mother's instinct told her to shout out, "Stop the car, Ethan!"

The car slowed to a stop, and Marilyn opened her door as soon as the brakes clicked. She rushed into the parking lot and scooped up the object she had seen. It was a good luck trinket Ophelia had received from her mother many years before. "Ethan, it's Ophelia's cross!" Marilyn shouted to him. "Pull in over here!"

As Ethan drove the car into the lot and parked, Marilyn started searching around for more clues. Looking for anything out of place, Marilyn zeroed in on a wide-open door in the apartment complex and started moving toward it. "Where are you going?" Ethan called out as he exited the car.

Marilyn refused to even acknowledge her husband as she sprinted across the parking area. Every instinct inside her screamed that something was wrong with her daughter and that her daughter had to be inside the apartment with the wide-open door. She charged through the door, prepared to fight off a dozen men if she had to. Instead, she found only Ophelia, curled up on a bed.

Ophelia's belly expanded once, letting Marilyn know she was alive. But her lips had begun to turn blue. "Ophelia!" Marilyn cried out. "Ophelia, please wake up!" She began to shake her daughter.

Ethan heard his wife's screams and ran for the apartment without hesitation. By the time he had called for an ambulance, neighbors were poking their heads out their doors and milling about in the parking lot, trying to get a look at what was going on. Marilyn continued to shake Ophelia, but her daughter wouldn't wake up.

Ethan had to rush outside to hear the dispatch operator as Marilyn raised another terrified scream to the heavens. Every second waiting for the ambulance seemed like an eternity to him, and his blood pressure skyrocketed as the voice on the other end faded in and out against the traffic rushing by. "She's still alive!" Marilyn screamed from inside the apartment. "Tell them to hurry!"

Finally, the wail of an ambulance siren over the traffic told Ethan that help was on the way. When the ambulance screeched into the parking lot, Ethan fell to his knees and thanked God. The paramedics pulled a stretcher through the open apartment door and wasted no time securing Ophelia to it and ushering her into the back of the ambulance. By now, police officers had arrived and had to restrain Marilyn to keep her separated from her daughter while the paramedics did their work.

"Don't let her die!" Marilyn screamed. "Please don't let her die!" Having freed herself from the officers, she immediately jumped into the Carters' car. "Come on, Ethan!" she called to her husband.

Ethan, who had been watching in a trance-like state as the scene played out in front of him, snapped out of it and practically dove into the driver's seat of the car. As the ambulance pulled out of the parking lot, Ethan and Marilyn followed as close behind as they could.

Chapter 43

OPHELIA FELT HOT DUST hitting her face. She didn't know how long she'd been unconscious, only that the falling dust was disturbing her slumber. The first thought in her mind was gratitude that she could sense her body again. Her deep-seated fear that she was already dead faded into the back of her mind.

Ophelia's dry lips peeled apart until an ember got inside her mouth. She gagged in shock at the burning heat of the ember. The gorge rose in her throat, and she tried to swallow it back down. Ophelia realized she was on her back because the bile floated back up. She raised her head. A blazing pain in her neck woke her up more, and she opened her eyes.

Overhead, there was a storm of dark clouds with purple lightning shooting through them. Iron-rich red dust obscured the sun and blew through the air, leaving crimson trailers. Four shattered brick walls, appearing to be the remnants of a house, framed this blistered sky. But the sky looked the same in every direction, having a horrible red glow.

Bricks falling from the walls pinned Ophelia's arms and legs to the ground. Some of the falling bricks were broken off at odd angles, but the ones pinning her arms down were fully intact. Pushing with all her might, Ophelia heard things clatter.

As she broke free from the bricks, her returning circulation made her extremities prickle with pain. Standing up was more of a challenge, between the persistent nausea and the dizziness. But Ophelia eventually managed to push herself upright and stagger away from the wall.

Ophelia tried to breathe deeply and take in her surroundings, looking for something she might recognize. *I know I'm inside a nightmare, but how did I end up there?* As she searched for answers, she wondered if her mind being forever trapped in a nightmare meant her body and life were in danger in the real world. Until now, Ophelia had always been a willing participant in other people's nightmares. Being trapped in one was a new threat.

A deep sense of urgency pushed Ophelia forward from the inside. Fear made her look for anything within the ruined world around her that would help her survive longer. But as she stepped beyond the ruined frame of the house, she was simply introduced to new horrors.

Fields of debris and collapsed buildings surrounded Ophelia while downriver, a bridge was collapsing segment by segment. Three segments had already fallen into the river below, but the large, bell-shaped counter-spans still arched above the water. With the bridge down, water, food, and any other kind of comfort seemed out of reach to Ophelia as she continued to wander the nightmare.

In the desolate landscape, Ophelia noticed other people wandering around, too. But none of them seemed to notice her—not even the ones nearby. She couldn't tell what was wrong with them, but something was making them wander

around. Huge monsters, three times as tall as humans, sauntered around the crowds of people. But Ophelia noticed that the
people seemed blind to the monsters' presence. Even with the
monsters walking right in front of them, the people showed no
reaction, only a dazed stagger.

Whatever caused the destruction around Ophelia had left
massive holes in the dirt that used to be basements and storm
shelters. One storm shelter stood close enough for Ophelia to
see its bottom. But it wasn't the bottom anymore. Beneath the
storm shelter flowed a river of molten lava, and every other
hole she could see had the same red glow that the lava gave off.
She had read about things like this coming from volcanoes and
supervolcanoes, but knowing what it was didn't diminish the
terror of seeing it firsthand.

On the far riverbank, lava leaked into the Missouri River,
sending a cone of steam downriver. That side of the river bore
small plumes of mist as well. One wanderer walked straight
over the edge of the storm shelter, right down the glowing hole.
And Ophelia suddenly realized that all the people around her
were blind. She had expected an earth-rending scream from the
person who fell, but no sound escaped them. "They're sleepwalking," Ophelia said aloud. Blind and deaf, the people
seemed entranced and oblivious, caught in some deeper nightmare or some wild daydream.

Stumbling across a theater, Ophelia hoped to find leftover
snacks or maybe a coat from a coat check. The dress that had
accompanied her on this nightmarish journey had large rips
from the bricks and burns from the embers, so she hoped to
find something that would cover her up. She suddenly realized

that the theater was just a burnt-out shell, with only its roof and façade left standing. But she nevertheless found a coat tucked into one remaining folding seat.

Ophelia thought it ironic to be wearing a coat while surrounded by lava, but logic seemed to have ceased amidst the end of the world. After putting the coat on, she searched through the concession stands, but they yielded nothing. Each glass case had already been broken and looted. The popcorn machines had shattered, and the vending machines were knocked over. Empty candy boxes and wrappers littered the floor.

The river became a destination and a distraction from the carnage. Ophelia abandoned the ghostly remains of the theater and made her way across the ground, following the path with the fewest cracks until she reached the bridge. Looking at the landscape around her made Ophelia's heart race. The searing winds made her squint, and as she squinted, the ashes and dust on her eyelashes made her eyes feel like they were burning.

As Ophelia pinched herself on the arm, a power line snapped in the air above her and fell to the ground, popping and crackling in the river's water. Ophelia dodged to one side as the power line fell, but she felt shooting pains in her feet before she could clear the water. One by one, every escape route Ophelia had was being blocked. Pete's nightmare was trying to keep her there forever.

Suddenly, Ophelia noticed firefighters trudging through Pete's nightmare, and she watched them as they made their way down to the river. There, she was shocked to see her own car bobbing up and down as it was slowly towed from the water with a tow chain. High above it, a Ford Explorer sat damaged in the bridge access lane. With cracked pavement and lava flows all around her, Ophelia realized that Pete's reality was still meshing with his nightmare, and it was all playing out in front of her.

If the real world can break through into Pete's nightmare, then perhaps his nightmare can seep into the real world! Ophelia reasoned with horror. The idea of this monstrous nightmare turning Earth into a lava-riddled disaster drove her panic even higher. Terrifying her further was that nobody in the real world or nightmare world seemed to see her or notice her, confirming that she was either stuck between worlds or . . . *Am I dead?* she wondered.

Ophelia approached Pete's Explorer and saw that he was still sitting inside. His eyes were closed, he had labored breathing, and blood was seeping through his shirt. Ophelia figured that he must have broken ribs. But as long as the blood was seeping, his heart must still be beating, she figured. "He's unconscious!" she heard someone shout from behind her. Paramedics were running toward the Explorer, but to Ophelia, it was all playing out in slow motion.

The paramedics tried Pete's door, but it wouldn't budge. As the Jaws of Life were prepared, Ophelia turned back to her own car, which had now been fully removed from the water. She was frozen in terror, fully expecting to see her own body in the car. But as the first responders pulled open the driver's side door and brown water poured out, Ophelia could see that it was David's body in the seat.

David's body had swollen during the drowning. He had inhaled so much water that his torso swelled to twice its normal size. Even his arms had grown beyond their normal size. And under his skin, a light blue tone spoke of all the water his muscles had absorbed before death.

Slowly piecing together what had happened, Ophelia realized that Pete's car must have collided with her own, sending David to his fate. "This is all my fault!" she cried out. "David is dead because of me tampering with Pete's nightmares!" Ophelia felt an immense wave of guilt and grief, followed by a sudden realization. *If the real world and nightmare world have combined, maybe I can find myself asleep on David's bed!*

Chapter 44

O PHELIA SCANNED THE LANDSCAPE, looking for landmarks she recognized. But this new combined real world and nightmare world was confusing. The volcanoes that were erupting in Pete's nightmare were on her side of the bridge when, in reality, the hills outside Branson were on the other side of the bridge. *It's a mirror image!* Ophelia realized. She was suddenly able to orient herself enough in Pete's nightmare to know which way to navigate through it.

Stumbling around on cracked pavement, with sulfuric wind burning against her feet, Ophelia slowly made her way toward where she thought David's apartment must be in Pete's nightmare world. But having few landmarks along the way due to the destruction made the apartment building difficult to find. Luckily, the distinctive wrought-iron gate outside David's apartment had survived the carnage, allowing Ophelia to navigate herself the rest of the way there.

Although David's apartment building also remained standing, the inside of his apartment was in shambles. Light streamed through dozens of holes in the ceiling, and Ophelia was dismayed to discover that his bed and mattress had been tossed up against the wall as though someone had ransacked the place. She pulled hard against the bedframe, trying to bring the mattress down to see if her body was on the other side.

As Ophelia wiggled and pulled the bed with all her might, a wooden beam broke free in her hand. But using one foot against the wall as leverage, she was eventually able to pull the entire bed and mattress down off the wall. Although she expected to see her body on the other side, instead, nothing was on the mattress but rust stains and blackened holes from flying embers.

Ophelia sat down on the mattress, confused and distraught. She wanted to solve the conundrum of where her body was so she could escape Pete's nightmare and return to the real world. But as she sat, her legs started cramping, and as she rubbed at the cramps, her hands became sore. More and more cramps came, increasing in intensity as burning embers singed her skin. Pete's nightmare was beginning to take its toll and weaken her.

Gazing through a massive hole in the wall, Ophelia saw the monsters still roaming the streets of Pete's nightmare version of Branson. Then, she was shocked to see David stumbling down the ruined pavement, coming toward the apartment. She was sure she had seen him dead, but there he was, alert and breathing. She had come back to life from drowning as a little girl. Was it possible Pete had incorporated that into his nightmare and brought David back, too?

Ophelia's joy at seeing David alive was quickly replaced by panic as she wondered whether this was some nightmare version of David coming to find her and enact revenge for killing him. She felt her jaw rattling beyond her control as the panic took hold. She grabbed her chin with her hand, forcing it to stop chattering. David spotted the movement at once. He stopped walking and stared straight at her.

David maneuvered around the remaining obstacles in his pathway. A crack had formed in the apartment's lot, and David jumped over the large gap, landing in a heap on the other side. His bloated gut bounced as he landed, and his arms flopped. Muddy river water was expelled from his body. Ophelia could now see that he was still a swollen corpse, confirming her fears. She half hoped he would not get up, but he quickly collected himself and continued moving toward her.

As David entered his apartment, Ophelia could see something wild glowing within his eyes, but it was just hollow glints in the distance. Marching forward, David closed the distance between him and Ophelia. Ophelia stood up from the bed as best she could and shuffled a few steps, ready to try a quick escape if she had to.

Stopping, David said, "Ophelia, I'm sorry. I couldn't wake you up. I tried to wake you, but I couldn't do it."

"It's all right, David," Ophelia reassured him. "It's not your fault that I'm here. Don't worry about it."

"It's *not* all right, Ophelia!" David shrieked in a voice that did not sound like his. Ophelia stumbled backward, knocking more bricks loose from the wall. As she wiggled a foot to remove a fallen brick from it, David screamed again, "It's not ok! You shouldn't have returned here! Now, Perkele has you in his lair!"

"Who's Perkele?" Ophelia asked.

"The demon that's going to end the world!" David shouted. "I've said too much! Help me! Please!" The glowing in David's eyes intensified. He screamed and crumpled to the floor in a heap. After a moment of convulsing and pounding his fists against the floor as though he were in tremendous pain, David slowly rose again. His eyes were now deep red embers, but the face looking at Ophelia was no longer his.

Chapter 45

"YOU'RE MINE NOW, Ophelia!" the creature standing in front of her shouted in the most warped and sinister voice Ophelia had ever heard. The creature's maroon eyes, full of blood and hatred, revealed his demonic nature. Ophelia wondered what else lurked beneath his discolored, stretched skin that had once been David's.

"Don't you know who I am by now?" the creature asked. "Did my vessel on Earth, David, not reveal anything about me to you?"

"You're Perkele!" Ophelia shouted. "I recognize your voice. You tried to drown me as a child. And now, you're trying to drown me in Pete's nightmare. Without my healing powers, you can end the word with endless pain and suffering."

"And there's no way to stop me now, Ophelia. I am a God, even if you see me as a demon. I am the God of destruction. My world of destruction, the one you call nightmares, is stronger than your world. My world is already increasingly breaking through to yours. You saw it with Isobel, you saw it with Hannah, and now, you see it with Pete. Soon, your world will be overrun with nightmares and will end."

"No, you're wrong," Ophelia shot back. "My world is protected by a loving, healing God. That God would never let you destroy everything He created!"

"Look around you, Ophelia," Perkele continued. "I've tried to show you what I'm capable of, with these rivers of lava, these ash-filled skies, and people too lost in their own nightmares to see what's happening around them. Do you need more proof that I am just as much a God as yours? Even as we speak, I am sending more shadows to your world to plant fresh nightmares and feed off the fear of those I've claimed."

"Is this all you can do? Turn a couple of nightmares into reality? If this is your masterpiece, you need more practice," Ophelia mocked him.

"You don't seem to understand that you're trapped in my world forever. Your body from the real world is gone. You're never going to escape." By now, an entire wall of David's apartment had crumbled. Perkele looked across it to the monsters roaming the streets and called out to them, "Come get her!"

Ophelia heard the horrendous sound of dozens of monsters shrieking as they turned their heads to look at her and began clawing their way toward the ruined apartment building. Her panic turned into an urgency that pounded in her head and told her she needed to run . . . now! *Perkele's right*, Ophelia realized. *How am I going to escape this nightmare if I can't find my body?*

Ophelia realized that Perkele had no real power to hurt her unless she was afraid of him, but she wasn't so certain about the monsters. Refusing to succumb to fear, she summoned all of her strength and aggression and glared at Perkele.

"You wouldn't hurt David, would you?" Perkele asked,

transforming into David's bloated corpse and using David's voice.

"You're not David!" Ophelia shouted. And with that, she shoved the bloated body in front of her out of the way and began to run without looking back. Escaping into the streets, she ran across pavement littered with cracks, jumping from time to time to avoid them. She hoped the cracks and fissures would slow the monsters behind her down, but instead, they effortlessly navigated the cracks, leaping from plate to plate of concrete in pursuit of Ophelia.

Beyond the roads, Ophelia founds waves of sand where the grasslands used to be. Sucking sounds and red, belching craters told her of a dangerous passage. Ophelia had difficulty running through the sand, but she figured the monsters would, too. Instead, the monsters seemed to move faster than ever, closing the gap to get to her. Making matters worse, Ophelia's legs continued to cramp. She knew she couldn't take much more.

As Ophelia approached a rocky hillside, she heard Perkele scream, "Get her!" He was no longer bothering to disguise his voice as David's. Ophelia collapsed, unable to go any further, and she hung her head, preparing for the end.

When Ophelia lifted her head for what she thought would be the final time, she noticed that the rock in front of her was no ordinary rock. The rock was glowing and pulsating with a familiar light, and the monsters seemed to slow their advance as they approached it. *Someone's trying to help me*, Ophelia realized. The thought alone was comforting to her.

Ophelia was certain that Paivatar had found her way into Pete's nightmare. She could think of no one else who would be helping her. It had been a long time since she had seen Pai-vatar's brilliant light, but yes, of course . . . it was unmistakable. With renewed strength and hope, Ophelia rose from the ground, squared her shoulders, and scrambled up the hillside.

When Ophelia reached the top of the hill, she noticed even stranger things. There were thick tubes pulsating across the glowing surface of the rocks. And deep inside the tubes, red lines seemed to thread through them. "This is part of Pete Reed's brain," Ophelia said out loud, shocked that she hadn't realized it before.

Inside Pete's nightmare, his brain had taken the form of a hill. Ophelia remembered finding Pete unconscious in his car and realized that if she didn't heal him, she might die along with him. Her hands began to glow. As she reached down with both hands and touched the tubes, she felt her energy transfer into the rocks.

The rocks representing Pete's brain glowed brighter, fed by Ophelia's healing energy. She became so caught up in healing Pete's brain that she completely forgot about the monsters chasing her until one of them clawed viciously across her abdomen, producing a gaping wound. Having nothing to fight the monster with, she continued healing Pete's brain and was astonished to see that the more she healed him, the further the monsters got from her. The monsters screaming below Ophelia—realizing they couldn't get to her—created a cacophony on the wind.

"Ophelia!" Perkele screamed over the cacophony. "I know you can hear me! This useless body is too bloated to climb the rocks, but I know you're up there. You can't hide forever!"

Resorting to crude methods, Ophelia tore off a piece of her clothing and used it to wrap the wound to her midsection. Then, she pressed her hands tighter to Pete's brain and delivered every last ounce of healing energy she could to it. But the combination of the wound and the release of energy caused Ophelia to feel dizzy. Her legs went akimbo, and she plummeted off the side of the rocks but managed to use one hand to grab on to a tube. Hanging suspended from the tube, Ophelia could feel herself losing control of her body and slipping downward. Raw fear threatened to drag her into madness as she resisted falling further from the rocky hillside.

Reaching up and gripping the tube with her other hand, Ophelia pulled herself back onto the rocks, then made her way to a sandy landing point on the other side of the hill. There, she prayed with all her might. "Paivatar, please hear my cries!" she shouted. She knew that Perkele was still lingering with the monsters and might hear the name of her angel, but she didn't care anymore. Ever since she had met David, that loving, comforting presence she knew as Paivatar had been missing from her life. "Please come back to me, Paivatar!" Ophelia begged.

Chapter 46

"YOU DON'T REALLY think that's going to work, do you?" Perkele called out to Ophelia. "Paivatar can't hear you. You're in *my* world now, remember?"

As Perkele was speaking, a golden light emerged from the sand, and Ophelia saw the grains shift and spiral as an energy built up. Slowly, a tower of light stretched into the sky and filled the air with a golden hue. "All you had to do was pray, child," a familiar voice echoed from above. "I've been right here with you the whole time."

"Who is that talking to you?" Perkele screamed louder than ever. Ophelia looked up and saw that Perkele had managed his way up the rocks. His bloated, evil face was now staring down at her from the top of the rocky hill. But with Paivatar by Ophelia's side, she no longer felt intimidated. "You can't be here!" Perkele shouted at Paivatar. "You can't be in my realm! It's forbidden!"

Paivatar looked up at Perkele. "You're done, Perkele. Get out of my sight." Faced with the power of a real God, Perkele had no choice but to back further away. He backed so far down the rocky hillside that Ophelia and Paivatar could no longer see him.

"He's coming back, isn't he?" Ophelia asked.

"Once he gathers enough strength, yes, he'll be back. Perkele is the master of chaos, and his apocalypse has been burning for centuries. Hundreds of years have passed since this nightmare Pete is having was first spawned. It's pulled countless victims into its wake. You are just its latest prize."

"But this nightmare is Perkele's domain. What does this have to do with me? I had nothing to do with creating this nightmare of the apocalypse."

"Oh, but you did, child," Paivatar informed Ophelia. "You are very much responsible for this. Don't you remember? Pete was just going about life as usual until *you* were about to give him a nightmare. That's the only reason you're here and vulnerable to Perkele."

"I strayed from healing, it's true. But only after you left me. Why did you leave me? You promised you would never leave."

"I never *did* leave! That demon, Perkele, got hold of you as soon as you touched David. From that moment on, I couldn't reach you until you prayed to me. When you started casting nightmares, you messed with things you didn't understand. Perkele gave you that power when you touched David. But you're the one who used it."

"I was angry!" Ophelia cried. "People were taking their healthy lives for granted and hurting everyone around them without paying for it! I had to do something!"

"It's precisely that thinking that has led to the endangerment of the very fabric of the world and of the very God who gave you your healing powers. You gave a lot of power to this nightmare not long ago. Remember that day you tried to give

Pete a new nightmare? This nightmare of the apocalypse was already happening in Pete's mind. It's a nightmare that's been tormenting him for decades. But when you started messing with his dream, the nightmare became even more powerful. The nightmare used your abilities to come into *your* world. Perkele has been trying to push through to your world for thousands of years. He's terrorized countless people with nightmares through the centuries, trying to enter your world. And by using you and your powers, he was finally able to do so."

"Why is Perkele using me? Shouldn't he be afraid of me?"

"When David came into your world, you stopped using your healing powers for good and started using them for evil, causing them to diminish and me to go away. So, Perkele was no longer afraid of you. But now that your healing powers have been restored, yes, you're a serious threat to him! You have enough power to destroy this nightmare and Perkele for good—*forever*."

"Yes, of course. I have to destroy this nightmare," Ophelia repeated out loud to herself.

"But Perkele has already used you to break through to your world. If you don't stop him now by destroying this nightmare, then he will just continue breaking through to the real world. Once he does that, this nightmare—the apocalypse—becomes a reality. Streets will crack, lava will flow, embers will rain from the sky, and everyone and everything will *die*! I gave you your healing powers back so you can stop him, not wallow in doubt. Have a little faith!"

Ophelia felt a strange tugging sensation, and she realized it was Paivatar pulling at her. The nightmare began to twist, bulge, and warp like a bubble being poked at. "What are you doing to me, Paivatar?" Ophelia asked.

"What you're about to see should give you some extra motivation to destroy this nightmare. I can tell you need it."

Ophelia's eyes went blurry, and she felt ice-cold. Rubbing her eyes back into focus, she realized she was in a hospital.

Chapter 47

T HE FRIGID HALLWAYS OF the hospital were a rude
contrast to the sweltering heat of Pete's nightmare.
"What are you doing to me, Paivatar?" Ophelia asked. "Why
am I here?"

"So that you can see what happened to you," Paivatar explained.

"Am I out of the nightmare?" Ophelia asked.

"I already told you how to stop the nightmare. This is just a
chance to find extra strength for doing so. Go through the door
by the elevator," Paivatar instructed.

Ophelia willed her eyesight through the door. On the other
side, she finally laid eyes on the body she had been seeking out
for what had felt like an eternity. Ophelia's body lay isolated in
an intensive care unit bed. She knew what the room was immediately, having stood in dozens of them during her years of
healing. But she had never expected to see her own body in one.

Ophelia's body was strapped to the ICU bed, and a number
of small tubes pumped fluids and medicines into her. It was
hard for Ophelia to look at her body in the condition it was in.
Bandages covered the gash in her abdomen, but the wounds
still looked horrific. She was shocked to see that an injury she
had sustained in the world of the nightmare had penetrated

through to her physical body in the real world. The two worlds had begun to merge even more than she realized.

The thing Ophelia had never gotten used to when looking at patients—the really bad ones—was the feeding tubes and the tracheotomy tubes forced into their nonresponsive mouths by doctors insistent on preserving their lives. The feeding tube shoved down her own throat, feeding her like a potted plant, was one thing. But the airway tube, pushed through a now-healed gash in her throat, left her reliant on machines for her survival. She was like one of those robots she read about in pulp magazines when she was young; she seemed part human, part machine.

"I don't want to be dependent on anyone!" Ophelia shouted. "I'm a healer, not a patient!" As Ophelia spoke, each pump of the oxygen tank lifted her body's ribcage, and her heart continued to thump, raising the skin by her throat—the skin that had not been damaged by the tube. "How could they do this to me?" she asked.

"Your parents are trying to save your life, Ophelia."

"But I'm so much better at it than they are!"

"That's the spirit, child! We're here to remind you of your desire to heal people—to remind you of how good it made you feel to use your healing powers. If you can destroy Pete's nightmare, you will free all people from all nightmares in one fell swoop of healing. Think about how good that will make you feel!"

"Yes, but I want to heal *her*, too," Ophelia said meekly as she gestured to her body. "If I could just touch her, I could make it all better."

"Don't even think about it," Paivatar warned. "You're still in the nightmare. If you touch your real-world body, you will undo everything. The nightmare will immediately rush into your body and into this world and destroy them both."

"This is not helping; this is torture!" Ophelia cried out.

"No, it's motivation to end the nightmare! We're going back there *now*."

"Why? You saved me when I was on death's door be-fore—when I was drowning. Why can't you do it again now? Why can't *you* just make it all stop?"

"Now is not the time for petulance, Ophelia! The universe needs you!"

As Ophelia reluctantly and silently nodded her agreement, the hospital walls started bulging toward her. She felt the strange tugging sensation again as she was pushed back into the nightmare. Suddenly, she was standing right back in the sandy spot at the bottom of the rocky hill that was Pete's brain.

"Seeing that was terrible!" Ophelia said. "That was like a nightmare inside a nightmare."

"Would you have let me show you if I had told you where we were going?"

"No, I suppose not. But how am I supposed to destroy this nightmare for good?" Ophelia asked. "You said that Perkele has been spreading this nightmare about the apocalypse for centuries. Where did the nightmare come from to begin with?"

"All nightmares are born of fear. And the fear of the end of the world is an ancient one, going back hundreds of thousands of years. For the first humans, the end of the world was a very real threat. They relied on the planet for their very survival—

for their nutrition, for their water, and for their other basic needs. This planet was all they had, and they knew it. You have no idea what you've unleashed by tampering with Pete's nightmare. Perkele knew you were powerful, and when he gave you the power to give humans nightmares, he was using you as a conduit to feed off people's fears and spread this nightmare."

"Where do I concentrate my healing energy to get rid of this nightmare?"

"Every nightmare is made of and feeds off fear. And every *good* dream is made of and feeds off hope. Destroy the root of Pete's fear, and the world will be free of this nightmare for good." Paivatar's words were enough to give Ophelia profound comfort. "Now, go end this, child. I won't let Perkele hurt you!"

Everything around Ophelia warned her to be afraid: the shifting sand, the flaming fissures, and the violent sky. But everything inside her felt opposite to her surroundings. She felt harmony and contentment, and healing energy flowed inside her. She had missed that feeling, and she relished its return.

Ophelia climbed the rocky hill that was Pete's brain once more. As she climbed, she inhaled hot ashes and toxic volcanic fumes and found it difficult not to cough. Putting both hands on the rock with the tubes and the red veins throbbing through it, she willed all her healing energy into it. Wave after wave of healing energy poured into the rock.

As the rock began to throb, Ophelia sensed the fear deep within it, and she tried to concentrate her energy toward the fear. She had never been charged with this much healing energy before. It stirred every fiber of her creation and filled her with glowing light. Paivatar must have been close by because Ophelia could feel a near-constant current of healing light pouring into her, replacing what she was using up on the creature.

Deep inside the rock, something glowed between the throbbing veins. The rock's red exterior marred to a purple glow as something blue came to life inside it. Ophelia tried to keep herself calm and tried to focus on pouring healing energy into the rock, but whatever was coming to life inside of it disrupted her attention. For a moment, Ophelia's energy streams faltered. She felt overwhelmed with compassion for the poor creature inside the rock whose only weapon was fear.

Regaining her focus, Ophelia continued the process of healing Pete's brain and destroying the source of his fear. As her energy penetrated deeper and deeper into the rock, it started to come into contact with whatever was shining blue. Suddenly, Ophelia could see clearer than ever, and in her mind, it was as if the veins of the rock had pulled away and she could see clear through the rock as though it were glass.

Deep inside the rock, Ophelia's mind could see a jet-black mass. This sucking black hole sat inside a deep vacuum—a place devoid of all light. Ophelia's healing energy surged into this light-deprived place. When the light smashed into the surface of the black mass, the fear peeled back. The deep mass of fear bubbled and tore as the golden light pounded into it, but it refused to shrink. Surrounded by darkness for so long, the mass could not comprehend the light and tried to evade it, pushing this way and that, surging in every direction to avoid illumination.

Ophelia tried to focus on keeping her hands in place on the rock while at the same time trying to make sense of the surges of sensations pouring into her mind. She succeeded in keeping her hands steady on the rock at all times, but she could see that the work was only half complete. Without a way to diminish the black mass, she was in a stalemate with it.

Feeling compassion again, Ophelia reached out to the dark mass with her heart, along with her healing energy. Her compassion was stronger than fear, and even through her mind's eye, she could see how much stronger her healing power became when compassion was added to the mix. Ophelia took pity on the fearful thing, and the black mass began to tear apart in shreds every time the light hit its surface. But even as it tore into shreds, the mass kept fighting to evade Ophelia.

Ophelia tried to stay aware of her surroundings, but the more she focused on destroying the fear, the less attention she paid to the desert around her. Eventually, she turned all her attention to the surface of the rock. The faster she could destroy this thing, the sooner she would be free of the nightmare. The more she kept blasting the dark thing with compassion and healing energy, the smaller it became, and the more Ophelia knew that she was winning the battle.

Suddenly, a strange violet glow settled over the dark mass, enhancing Ophelia's light. She knew that Paivatar was still helping her. Their combined energy drove light deeper into the darkness, where it pierced in the deepest and purest darkness of true fear, trying to snuff it out. Ophelia knew the fear was weakening, but she had never seen a fear as powerful as the one in Pete's brain. It festered and boiled no matter how long it was pounded with healing light. At the center, the fear was still jet-black, unaffected by the healing light around it.

"It's all right!" Ophelia called out to the dark fear inside the rock. "There's nothing to be afraid of! It's just light!"

"No! Don't do it!" Perkele suddenly screamed. Seemingly out of nowhere, his bloated, evil body came climbing up the rocks, grabbing at Ophelia's ankles.

Knowing she could not fight Perkele directly, Ophelia pushed all the energy she could muster into the rock and toward the dark mass of fear. "You're afraid," Ophelia said with the deepest reverence. "It's okay," she said. "You don't have to be afraid anymore. That ends today."

Ophelia heard snapping sounds, and suddenly, she could no longer see through the rock. She looked down at the rock, and it seemed as boring and plain as a normal rock. Then, she could barely see the rock at all as it faded into darkness. More loud snaps and then popping sounds preceded complete blackness. Everything had gone dark.

"Paivatar?!" Ophelia called out. But there was no answer. Blinded, panicked, and feeling weak and in need of rest, Ophelia crossed her legs and tried to sit down. That's when she realized there was nothing to sit on. She began to have the sensation of falling, but instead of making her fearful, she felt at peace.

Chapter 48

O PHELIA FELT FREEZING COLD and opened her eyes at once. Above her was a dull, white light, and Ophelia quickly realized that she was looking through the fibers of a sheet. She tore the sheet off as fast as she could and sat up. There were metal trays around her, and she grew more aware of an icy cold under her buttocks. She was naked except for the gauze around her wounds and the toe tag on her foot.

On the floor beside her, Ophelia saw that the morgue technician had passed out, but his chest was still moving up and down, letting her know he was ok. She also saw the wall of doors where bodies were slid in, including one door that hung wide open, waiting for Ophelia's body. A strange partial numbness in Ophelia's legs had been bothering her in Pete's nightmare, but she didn't connect it to being dead until now.

Ophelia stood up and began to walk. Every step made her gasp with cold until she spied a white lab coat on a hanger, grabbed it, and put it on. As she approached the exit from the morgue into the main hospital, she could see daylight streaming through a window. She pushed the double exit doors open, one with each hand, and was nearly blinded by the light that had been denied her since she had entered Pete's nightmare.

Ophelia stood in the hospital hallway, soaking up the sunlight streaming in from windows all around her. She felt alone and anonymous. Raising her hands before her and focusing with all her might, Ophelia tried to summon her healing energy. But not even the slightest flicker of light emerged from her hands. Ophelia could sense that her healing powers were gone forever. With Perkele's nightmare having been destroyed, the world was a better and safer place, and she was no longer needed for healing.

Although Ophelia enjoyed healing others, the pressure of doing so had become a huge burden in her life. She had increasingly desired to be free of the burden of being a healer and of being on display for the sake of her parents' desires for fame and fortune. Now, she had been set free. She was free to live the rest of her life the way she chose to live it.

The sky in the nightmare had been dark and threatening, but the sky outside the hospital was clear and bright blue. Ophelia spotted an exit door and moved toward it with determination, not caring about her bare feet or her toe tag. As she stepped close to the doors, they automatically wooshed open, and her bare feet felt a welcomed rush of cool air after having been trapped in a boiling nightmare for what had felt like years. Every sensation Ophelia was feeling was a benediction—a blessing—and she was already starting to feel excited.

Stepping into a grassy courtyard outside the hospital, Ophelia closed her eyes and felt the heat of a million rays of sunlight hit her face. "It's a good day," she said out loud. She couldn't stop enjoying the sunlight on her face if she wanted to. The light was a blessing to behold after so long trapped inside a sunless nightmare. Ophelia knew that nothing would ever steal her joy again.

"Ophelia?!" a woman's voice shrieked from behind her. Ophelia turned to find her parents, Marilyn and Ethan, exiting through the same door she had exited from. They had been on their way to the morgue, and they had tears in their eyes. "You're alive!" Marilyn shouted. "They told us you were dead! It's been a nightmare."

"Well, don't worry," Ophelia said, with a huge smile and a burst of optimism that surprised both of her parents. "No one will ever have nightmares again."

As Ophelia walked with her parents to their car, she locked eyes with a patient who was waiting in a wheelchair by the hospital's pickup lane. The corners of Pete Reed's mouth turned upward, and he delivered Ophelia a knowing nod.

From the Publisher

Thank You from the Publisher

Van Rye Publishing, LLC ("VRP") sincerely thanks you for your interest in and purchase of this book.

VRP hopes you will please consider taking a moment to help other readers like you by leaving a rating or review of this book at your favorite online book retailer. You can do so by visiting the book's product page and locating the button for leaving a rating or review.

Thank you!

Resources from the Publisher

Van Rye Publishing, LLC ("VRP") offers the following resources to readers and to writers.

For *readers* who enjoyed this book or found it useful, please consider receiving updates from VRP about new and discounted books like this one. You can do so by following VRP on Facebook (at www.facebook.com/vanryepub), Twitter (at www.twitter.com/vanryepub), or Instagram (at www.instagram.com/vanryepub).

From the Publisher

For *writers* who enjoyed this book or found it useful, please consider having VRP edit, format, or fully publish your book manuscript. You can find out more and submit your manuscript at VRP's website (at www.vanryepublishing.com).

Thank you again!

About the Author

MELISSA SAARI grew up in Butte, Montana, which is Evel Knievel's hometown, and Montana is the setting of her romance novel *Mystic Lake*. She graduated from Southern New Hampshire University with a Master of Arts and Literature, with a concentration in screenwriting. Melissa loves animals and has taken care of many cats and dogs, including her two current dogs, Marla and Leo. She loves dogs because of their loyalty and protectiveness, which are traits of the characters in Melissa's young adult novels *Curse of the Lion People* and *Curse of the Black Dragon* and her horror novels *The Red Satin Shoes* and *Blue Satin Diary*. Melissa currently lives in Central Washington, where the wild and mighty currents of the Columbia River flow past her door with an air of power and mysticism that further informs her writing.